DATE DUE		
SE 0 6 02		
OC 6 05		
AG 0 2 00		
SE 2 1 06		
NO 0 1 08		
DE 1 1 08		
AP 0 2 09		
JE 3 0 10		
MY 1 0		

Mandie® Mysteries

MANDIE®
AND THE
QUILT MYSTERY

Lois Gladys Leppard

BETHANY HOUSE PUBLISHERS
MINNEAPOLIS, MINNESOTA 55438

Mandie and the Quilt Mystery
Copyright © 2002
Lois Gladys Leppard

MANDIE® and SNOWBALL® are registered trademarks
of Lois Gladys Leppard.

Cover illustration by Chris Wold Dyrud
Cover design by Eric Walljasper

Published by Bethany House Publishers
A Ministry of Bethany Fellowship International
11400 Hampshire Avenue South
Bloomington, Minnesota 55438
www.bethanyhouse.com

Printed in the United States of America by
Bethany Press International
Bloomington, Minnesota 55438

ISBN 1-55661-676-7

Dear Mandie Readers:

At this time when our great nation is suffering, we the people feel helpless as to what to do next in our lives. The tragedies on September 11, 2001, cast a shadow of fear over our country and stabbed our hearts with pain.

However, God is still on His throne, watching over us. He will take care of us.

Remember Mandie's verse:

"What time I am afraid
I will put my trust in Thee."
Psalm 56:30

With love to you all,

Lois Gladys Leppard

Win a MANDIE BOOK!
See page 151.

About the Author

LOIS GLADYS LEPPARD worked in Federal Intelligence for thirteen years in various countries around the world. She now makes her home in South Carolina.

The stories of her mother's childhood as an orphan in western North Carolina are the basis for many of the incidents incorporated in this series.

Visit with Mandie at *www.Mandie.com*.

Contents

Acknowledgment

With many thanks to Stephanie Grace Whitson—author of the PRAIRIE WINDS series, DAKOTA MOONS series, and KEEPSAKE LEGACIES series—for sharing her expertise in quilt making.

Chapter 1 / Plans Are Made

Mandie Shaw was sitting in the swing on the long veranda, with Snowball curled up beside her, enjoying the fact that school was out. She had just arrived home the day before and was eagerly awaiting the arrival of her friends to begin their summer vacation together.

She glanced up and saw Dr. Woodard and Joe coming down the road in their buggy. Rushing down the walkway, she caught up with them as the doctor turned the vehicle into the lane to the backyard.

"Hello," Mandie called to them.

Dr. Woodard greeted her and turned to his son to say, "I'll take the buggy on around to the barn."

Joe jumped down, replying, "Thanks," and greeted Mandie with, "And hello to you."

Mandie looked up at Joe standing there and thought he must have grown at least six inches since spring holidays. And he seemed to be better looking every time she saw him. With these thoughts she suddenly became shy.

Joe ran his long fingers through his wavy brown hair and said with a big grin, "Cat got your tongue?"

"Oh, Joe Woodard, come on up on the porch," Mandie replied, quickly leading the way.

They sat in the swing as Snowball jumped down and ran out into the yard.

Joe looked around and asked, "When is Celia coming?"

"Today. She got out of school a week early because she had to go with her mother to Richmond to attend to some business," Mandie explained. "Mr. Bond has taken Uncle John's rig to go on several errands for him. He's supposed to get finished in time to meet the train, which should be any time now."

"Then when will we be leaving for New York?" Joe asked.

"Probably tomorrow," Mandie replied. She looked down the road and quickly stood up. "I believe that's Celia coming now." She stepped over to the banister as a horse-drawn vehicle came closer. "At least, it's Uncle John's rig, so Celia and her mother should be in it. And also Frances Faye, the girl we met during the tornado. Remember we asked her to come with Celia?"

"Yes, I definitely remember her. I wonder if she has ever found her grandmother," Joe said, joining Mandie at the banister.

The rig stopped at the gate to the road. Mandie hurried down the long walkway, and Joe followed.

Mrs. Hamilton stepped down to the stepping block with Celia close behind her. Mr. Bond, who worked for Mandie's uncle, began unloading their luggage. Joe went forward to help.

"Welcome, Mrs. Hamilton," Mandie greeted her. "Mother and Grandmother are in the parlor." Then she reached to hug her friend Celia.

"Thank you, Amanda. I'll go find them," Mrs.

Hamilton said, going on up the walkway to the front porch.

Mandie looked around and asked, "Did Frances Faye come with y'all?"

"No, Mandie," Celia replied with a big grin. "Because she found her grandmother and didn't want to leave her."

As Joe passed them, carrying two valises, he said, "I'm going to set these inside the front door and come back and help Mr. Bond with the trunks."

"You don't have to. There's Abraham coming across the yard to help," Mandie told him.

Abraham worked as a handyman for John Shaw, and Abraham's wife, Jenny, was the cook. They had both lived with the Shaw family for many years in their own cottage on the back of the property.

Joe stopped to call to Abraham, "I'll be right back to help with the other things."

"No never you mind," Abraham called back as he continued toward the rig. "Don't be needin' no help. Yo' papa lookin' fo' you."

"Thank you," Joe replied as he reached the front steps.

"Tell me about Frances Faye's grandmother," Mandie said to Celia, pushing open the screen door for Joe to go through with the luggage.

"It really wasn't hard at all to find her," Celia replied.

The girls entered the front hallway behind Joe, who deposited the valises by the hall tree.

Dr. Woodard, with John Shaw, was coming down the hallway.

"I was looking for you, son," Dr. Woodard told Joe. "I have to go up the mountain to see Mrs.

Collins. Her son has been down here today and left a message for me since he knew I'd be making calls around the area this week. She's not doing too well, so I may not be back until tomorrow. Depends on how things are in that area, whether anyone else is ill."

"Did you want me to go with you, Dad?" Joe asked.

"No, no, you stay here and get ready for your trip to New York with your friends," Dr. Woodard said. "I may not get back before y'all leave town."

"But you are still going with all of us to visit Mandie's Cherokee kinpeople after we get back from New York, aren't you?" Joe asked.

"Oh yes," Dr. Woodard told him. "I'll go home and get your mother and be here when you return from New York. Behave yourself and have a good time up there." He turned back down the hallway.

"Yes, sir," Joe replied.

John Shaw called after him, "I'll see that he behaves in New York." He laughed as he glanced at Joe. "Now, Miss Celia, we are glad to see you."

"Thank you, Mr. Shaw," Celia replied.

Abraham and Mr. Bond came in with Celia's trunk.

"Which room, missy?" Mr. Bond asked Mandie.

"My room. Celia is going to share my room with me," Mandie replied.

"And, Joe, your father and I put your bags in the first room on the left at the top of the staircase," John Shaw explained as he walked toward the parlor door.

"Thank you, Mr. Shaw," Joe said. Turning to the girls, he said, "While Celia is getting settled in your room, Mandie, I'll go on up and freshen up."

"Meet you in the back parlor in thirty minutes," Mandie told him.

Up in Mandie's room, the girls hung up Celia's dresses from her trunk as they talked.

"And how did Frances Faye find her grandmother?" Mandie asked, pushing her dresses to one end of the huge wardrobe to make room for Celia's.

"It so happened that Mrs. Edmonds, one of our neighbors, had heard of a lady by the name of Fordham who lived way out in the country on the other side of Richmond," Celia explained as she hung up a dress.

"So y'all went to investigate," Mandie said.

"Yes, Aunt Rebecca and I took Frances Faye in our rig and drove out in the direction Mrs. Edmonds had explained," Celia said. Then excitedly she added, "Oh, Mandie, you should have seen the old lady when she found out who Frances Faye was. We thought she was going to absolutely suffocate the girl, she hugged her so tight. And then Frances Faye began crying and couldn't speak for a few minutes. I wish you could have been with us."

"I do, too," Mandie agreed. "I'm so happy for her."

"And, Mandie, her grandmother must be wealthy," Celia said. "I want you to see her mansion someday. I think it's the biggest house I've ever seen. And the part I saw was furnished in stuff that must have cost a fortune."

"Celia, I wonder why Frances Faye's mother never had anything to do with the grandmother," Mandie said, frowning thoughtfully. "From what Frances Faye told us, her mother barely had a living, and they lived in an old house."

"I have no idea, Mandie. That's a mystery you'll have to solve," Celia said, hanging up the last of her dresses.

"Yes, I suppose I'll have to go visit Frances Faye in her new home someday," Mandie said.

When the girls joined Joe in the back parlor, they had to explain about Frances Faye and her grandmother.

"It's wonderful that Frances Faye was able to find her grandmother so quickly," Joe said. "I can imagine how she felt when her mother died and she had no one in this world."

"Yes, but I'm wondering why the mother and the grandmother never were in contact," Mandie said.

Joe shrugged his shoulders and said, "They probably didn't like each other for some reason."

"But I wonder why," Mandie said, squinting her blue eyes as she frowned in thought.

"Mandie, you might as well forget about poking into those people's business. It wouldn't be nice at all," Joe told her.

"If I go visit them, I wouldn't have to poke," Mandie answered with a big grin. "Frances Faye has probably found out by now why her grandmother and her mother never were in contact. And Frances Faye would probably just tell me without my asking."

At that moment someone tapped on the door and then opened it. Polly Cornwallis, Mandie's next-door neighbor and schoolmate, stuck her head inside. "I figured you'd all be back here," she said as she came into the room and sat down. "My mother is in the parlor visiting with your mothers." She looked at Mandie and Celia.

"Well, hello, Polly," Mandie said, not too happy

to see the girl. She always seemed to know when Joe was visiting at Mandie's house, and she would always find some excuse to come visit.

"My mother and I just arrived a little while ago," Celia remarked.

"And so did I," Joe added.

Everyone seemed at a loss for conversation.

"My mother came over to ask your mother, Mandie, if I could go to New York with y'all. Mother has other plans, so we thought it would be nice if I could join y'all. I'd just love to see that good-looking Jonathan Guyer again," Polly explained, all the time keeping her eyes on Joe.

Mandie felt her face flush in anger as she tried to steady her voice to keep Polly from knowing she was displeased with the idea of the girl traveling all the way to New York with them and then staying at Jonathan's house. She blew out her breath and said, "So my mother agreed?"

"Yes, she did. Isn't that wonderful?" Polly replied.

"We may be leaving tomorrow. Can you get ready that fast?" Mandie asked.

"Of course," Polly said. "The servants will pack my clothes for me."

"How long will your mother be gone?" Celia asked.

"She's not sure, but she said she'd let Mrs. Shaw know before we leave," Polly explained. "I'm so excited about the trip, especially the chance to see Jonathan's great mansion. Y'all had told me you could get lost in it, remember?"

"Yes, it is huge," Mandie agreed. "I can imagine there are lots of secret places in it."

"Secret places?" Polly questioned her.

"Yes, spooky, dark closets and attics and

basements where someone could hide," Mandie replied. She knew how afraid Polly was of even going into the basement at their boarding school or in the Shaw house.

"Hmm," Polly muttered as she shrugged her shoulders and tossed her long dark hair over her shoulder. She straightened up and said, "Well, we don't have to go poking into places like that."

"Not unless Mandie finds a mystery that we have to explore in such places," Joe said, grinning at Mandie.

"But we don't have to help Mandie solve mysteries up there, that is, if she finds any," Polly protested. She squinted her dark eyes.

"Oh, Polly, Mandie finds a mystery everywhere she goes," Celia said. "However, we don't have to help solve them if we don't want to."

"That's right," Mandie agreed. "You can stay by yourself while we go off solving mysteries in New York."

"I will make that decision when you actually find a mystery," Polly said. She stood up. "Now I have to go see if my mother is ready to go home." She started toward the door and added, "Mandie, your mother promised to let us know exactly when I should be ready to travel."

"We will, Polly," Mandie replied as Polly left the room and closed the door behind her.

"Whew!" Joe blew out his breath and said, "She probably won't join us in any mystery at Jonathan's house."

"We may not even find a mystery up there," Celia said.

"I just wanted her to know that if I do run into a mystery up there, I certainly plan on solving it," Mandie said.

The door opened right then, and Liza, the Shaws' young maid, stuck her head into the room and announced, "Dat Miss Sweet Thang has done gone home with her ma now." She grinned and closed the door.

"Thank you, Liza," Mandie said as the door closed. She stood up and said, "Let's go in the parlor and find out when we will be leaving for New York."

Celia and Joe followed Mandie out the door.

Mandie's mother, Elizabeth, her grandmother, Mrs. Taft, and Celia's mother were discussing their journey to New York.

"Y'all come on in," Elizabeth Shaw told them. "I believe we have our final plans made."

"Yes, ma'am," Mandie said, sitting on a settee with her two friends.

"We've decided we should go ahead tomorrow," Elizabeth said. "So y'all need to have your luggage ready for the train tomorrow."

"And bring enough clothes to last you two weeks. That's how long we will be staying in New York," Mrs. Hamilton said.

"And we had to invite that Polly Cornwallis to go with us," Mrs. Taft said with a loud sigh. "I do hope she doesn't spoil our visit for us."

"Don't worry, Grandmother, we won't let her," Mandie promised with a big grin. That was one thing they had in common. Neither of them was fond of Polly Cornwallis.

"I wouldn't be so sure of that," Joe whispered.

"I just hope the weather will be nice while we're there and that it doesn't rain," Elizabeth said.

Mrs. Hamilton laughed and said, "Somehow it always seems to rain when I visit up there."

Mandie asked, "We are all going to stay at the

Guyers' house, aren't we?'' She looked at her grandmother. Everyone knew Mrs. Taft didn't seem to be very friendly with Jonathan Guyer's father, and no one knew exactly why.

"Of course, dear, we've all been invited to stay there," Elizabeth replied.

Mandie looked at her friends and whispered, "Now, there's a mystery right there. If Grandmother doesn't like Mr. Guyer, why does she agree to go visit there?"

"You should find out," Joe whispered back teasingly.

"It would be something interesting to know," Celia also whispered.

"Amanda, have you sorted out what you plan on taking with you? If not, now is a good time to do it," Elizabeth said.

Mandie stood up and replied, "If Abraham could bring my trunk down from the attic, I could begin filling it up."

Joe instantly joined Mandie as he said, "Mrs. Shaw, I would be glad to get it down for her."

"Thank you, Joe, that would save some time," Elizabeth replied. "Amanda, show Joe where it is."

"Yes, ma'am," Mandie answered as she went out the door.

Joe and Celia followed as Mandie climbed the steps to the attic. She pushed open the door at the top of the stairs. It was dark inside the attic because all the shutters on the windows were closed, but Mandie knew exactly where her trunk was, which was not far from the door.

"If you'll get one handle, I'll get the other, and we can get it down the stairs," Mandie said, stooping to reach for the handle on one end.

Joe got the other handle and said, "I could

probably get it by myself by sliding it down the steps if it's empty."

"It's empty, but I'll help anyway if you'll get in the front so you can catch the weight if I drop my end," Mandie told him.

"All right, but please let me know if you are going to turn it loose. Those steps are steep, and it could get out of control," Joe warned her.

"And I will stay behind y'all just in case," Celia told them.

They were about halfway down the steps when Snowball came running up to them, slipped by, and went on through the attic door. The three stopped to look.

"Oh shucks, now I'll have to go get that cat," Mandie said, looking back up the steps. "I forgot to close the door."

"I could see if he will come to me, Mandie," Celia told her.

"He probably won't even come to me. I'll have to find him and carry him out of that attic. You know how much he loves to nose around up there," Mandie replied.

"Just let go of your end, Mandie. Since the trunk is empty, it's not heavy. I'll let it slide the rest of the way," Joe told her.

"I'll help you, Joe," Celia said, stepping down to take the handle Mandie was holding.

"All right, then. Y'all wait for me at the landing, and I'll go get Snowball," Mandie told them.

Mandie hurried back up, calling, "Snowball, Snowball, come here. Where are you?"

She slowly made her way through the darkness in the room, trying to spot the white cat as she called to him. There was no sound until she accidentally ran into an old lampstand, which turned over and made a loud noise. Then Snowball came flying out of the stuff stored there and raced out the door and down the steps.

"I don't think I broke anything," Mandie said to herself as she turned to leave the room. She closed the door behind her this time as she went down the stairs. She saw Snowball disappear at the foot of the steps.

Mandie caught up with her friends, who had the trunk all the way down to the floor below.

"Thanks," Mandie told them. "Since this is the third floor, all we need to do now is get it down one more flight of stairs." She reached for a handle.

Just as the three reached the second floor, where Mandie's room was, Mandie looked down the next flight and saw Uncle Ned, her father's old Cherokee friend, coming up.

"Oh, there's Uncle Ned," she told her friends.

As the three waited for the old man to get up the steps, Mandie noticed he was carrying some kind of bundle. Then she became excited as she went to meet him. "Oh, Uncle Ned, you've brought back the quilt we found in the attic during Christmas holidays," she said, looking at the bundle.

"Miz Lizbeth say bring quilt up here to Papoose," Uncle Ned said. "Where put it?"

"We can just put it in my room for the time being. What did the quilt say, Uncle Ned? Did you get the message written on it read?" Mandie was jabbering away without waiting for him to reply.

This was the quilt she and her friends had found in the attic and which Uncle Ned said contained a Cherokee message written on it. He had taken it home with him then and promised to get Uncle Wirt, the oldest member of the tribe, to translate the message.

Mandie led the way to her room, and everyone followed. Uncle Ned laid the quilt on her bed. She quickly unrolled it to look at the symbols sewn on it. "Well, Uncle Ned, what does it say?" she asked again.

Uncle Ned frowned as he stood there looking at the quilt. "Secret," he said, shaking his head sadly.

"A secret message? But what does it say, Uncle Ned? What did Uncle Wirt tell you it meant?" Mandie insisted.

Uncle Ned shook his head again. "Wirt say sad, bad message. Put quilt back where you find it," he said slowly.

"But, Uncle Ned, I want to know what the quilt says. Please," Mandie insisted.

"Wirt say no tell, sad, bad message," the old man repeated. He turned to leave the room.

Mandie suddenly stomped her foot and said, "Uncle Ned, please tell me what this quilt says."

The old man continued out of the room. Mandie followed him, with Joe and Celia right behind her.

When they got down to the first floor, Uncle Ned stopped and looked at Mandie. "No can tell, Papoose, sorry," he said.

"Well, if you won't tell me, I'll find someone who will tell me what that quilt says," Mandie told him. As he went on down the hallway, she sat down on the bottom step. Joe and Celia joined her.

"Mandie, I wonder why he wouldn't tell you," Celia said.

"It's just a silly old quilt with some silly message written on it," Joe added.

"But there's some reason he won't tell me what the message is, and I intend finding out. That quilt is so old it couldn't harm anyone to know what the message is," Mandie told her friends.

"What are you going to do, Mandie?" Celia asked.

"Why, I'll just ask some of my Cherokee kinpeople what it says," Mandie quickly decided. "They would be able to decipher all those symbols on it. That's what I'll do."

Chapter 2 / An Unexpected Ally

Joe sat on a low stool near the opened door of Mandie's bedroom and watched as the girls filled their trunks.

"You just unpacked your trunk a little while ago, and now you are having to repack everything," he told Celia.

Celia paused as she reached for a dress hanging in the wardrobe and replied. "But I'm not repacking everything, only the clothes I will need in New York. Remember, we are going to visit Mandie's Cherokee kinpeople when we come back, so I'll save some things for that journey."

Mandie looked up at her friend as she bent over her trunk to straighten the contents. "You won't need much for that visit," she reminded her. "We won't be socializing and all that like we will be in New York."

"Yes, and I'm so glad we won't be having to get dressed up and worrying about our hair and everything. It will be a pleasant time that we can really enjoy," Celia said.

"Enjoy?" Joe said with a grin, glancing at Mandie. "You mean if Mandie doesn't discover one of those complicated mysteries she's always running into."

"I don't have to run into a mystery this time. I already have one," Mandie told him. "I'm going to find out what the message on that quilt is." She suddenly straightened up and looked at her two friends as she excitedly added, "I have a idea. Why don't we go to visit my Cherokee kinpeople first and then go to New York later?"

"Oh, Mandie, your mother has already planned everything," Celia quickly reminded her.

"Besides, the Guyers are expecting us to arrive in the next few days," Joe added.

Mandie clasped her hands together and marched around the room as she frowned and mumbled to herself. "We could rearrange everything."

"No, Mandie, we have to go to New York tomorrow. I'm sure your mother will insist that we do," Joe said. "You know that."

"I'm not sure she will, and I won't know until I ask her," Mandie replied. "We could go with Uncle Ned tomorrow when he goes home. And it shouldn't take long to get someone to look at the quilt and tell me what those symbols on it mean. Then we could come on back and go to New York."

"It sounds simple, Mandie," Celia said. "But you know how your Cherokee kinpeople stick together on everything. If your Uncle Wirt refuses to tell you what the message is on the quilt, you may not find anyone who will dare tell you. After all, he is the oldest, and the others all respect him."

Mandie stopped pacing around the room, stomped her foot, and said, "Oh, that quilt was made many, many years ago, so what difference would it make if someone told me what it says? This is 1903, and Uncle Ned thinks that quilt was made around sixty or seventy years ago."

"And was packed away in your attic until we found it last Christmas," Celia said in amazement. "I wonder what else is up there that's old like that."

"We've been through so much of the stuff in the attic off and on that I don't imagine we've missed much of it," Mandie said. Looking at her friends, she asked, "Anyhow, Celia, Joe, would y'all agree to go visit my kinpeople first and then go to New York if I ask my mother about changing our plans? And please don't feel obligated to say yes if you don't really mean it."

"Whatever you want to do is fine with me, Mandie," Celia told her.

Joe ran his long fingers through his unruly brown hair and slowly answered, "Well, now, I don't really mind. However, we should think of the inconvenience for the other people involved."

"If I explain to everyone else about the quilt, I don't think they will get upset," Mandie said, and then with a big smile, she added, "Thank you both. I'll talk to my mother. I'll go find her right now." She started toward the door.

"Mandie," Celia called after her. "What about our trunks? Should I keep on packing my trunk?"

Mandie stopped at the doorway, turned, and replied, "Yes, Celia, keep putting whatever you want for New York in it, because if we go to see my kinpeople first, we'll only take a valise. We won't need the trunks."

Joe stood up and teased, "Oh, the trouble girls have with their clothes. I'm going to my room and putting mine in two piles, one for New York and one for the Cherokee visit. That way I'll be ready whatever the decision is."

"I'll be back as soon as I discuss things with my

mother," Mandie promised as she went out of the room.

Mandie went to the parlor, where she found her mother, Uncle John, and Uncle Ned. She looked around as she entered the room and asked, "Where is Grandmother? And Celia's mother?" She went to sit on a stool near her uncle.

"They've both gone to their rooms to sort out things for our journey tomorrow," Elizabeth Shaw told her daughter. "Are you finished with your packing?"

"Mother, that's what I came to talk about," Mandie began. She then turned to Uncle Ned and asked, "Are you going home tomorrow, Uncle Ned?"

"Yes, home, sun come up tomorrow," the old man replied.

Relieved to hear that he would be going home and not by the way of various other places he sometimes visited, Mandie glanced at her uncle John Shaw and then turned back to her mother. "Yes, ma'am, I think I have everything I need in my trunk. But, Mother, I wanted to ask you about changing our plans." She paused, not sure how to say things.

"Changing our plans?" Elizabeth quickly asked.

Uncle John looked at Mandie and asked, "Are you sick or something?"

"Or have you decided you just don't want to go to New York?" her mother asked. "Remember, Amanda, there are other people involved in these plans."

Mandie faintly smiled at her uncle and said, "No, sir, I'm not sick." Turning to her mother she said, "I've decided I'd like to go home with Uncle

Ned and visit my kinpeople awhile and then go to New York."

"Amanda, you know what our plans are, New York first and then to visit your kinpeople," her mother reminded her in a sharp voice. "You can't just change your mind at a minute's notice when it affects other people."

"What brought this on?" John Shaw asked.

Mandie felt Uncle Ned's gaze on her and believed that he had immediately figured out why she wanted to change her plans. And she was wondering if her mother and her uncle also realized this. Replying to John Shaw's question, she said, "Uncle Ned is here right now and is going straight home from here, so we could go with him now. But we don't know whether he will be here after we come back from New York for us to go with him then." She paused to take a breath.

"No, Amanda, we will be going to New York tomorrow as we have planned," her mother stated firmly. "So be sure you have your things ready. Mr. Bond will be taking our trunks to the depot tomorrow morning."

"But, Mother—" Mandie began.

"That is my final decision, Amanda," Elizabeth interrupted her. "Do you understand me?"

Mandie took a deep breath, stood up, and barely looked at her mother as she replied, "Yes, ma'am." She hurried out into the long hallway and went to sit on the bottom step of the staircase.

She had to get her breath and think things over for a few minutes before she went back upstairs to tell her friends they would be going to New York tomorrow as planned. She didn't have to go find them, however, because in a few minutes Joe and Celia came down the stairs.

Mandie didn't speak, and the two friends seemed to understand as they sat down next to her on the steps without a word.

Finally Mandie spoke. "We go to New York tomorrow," she said.

"All right," Celia said.

"I'll be ready," Joe told her.

"Guess I'd better finish packing my trunk," Mandie said as she stood up and started up the stairs.

Celia also rose, looked at Joe, and said, "We'll wait for you in the back parlor."

"Don't take too long," Joe teased.

Mandie didn't reply but went up the stairs and down the hallway to her room. All she could think of now was hurrying to get to New York and hurrying to get back home again and then hurrying to her kinpeople with the quilt.

Hastily snatching clothes down from the wardrobe, she piled them into the trunk until it wouldn't hold any more. Then she suddenly burst into tears and sat on the floor by the opened trunk. Snowball, who had been asleep in a chair, came to her side, purring loudly and rubbing against her shoes. Snowball had different kinds of purrs, depending on the situation, and this one was his purr where he sounded like he was trying to talk.

Mandie, suddenly giggling, reached to pick him up. She rubbed her face against his white fur. "All right, Snowball, I stopped crying," she whispered in his ear. She took a deep breath and stood up, holding the cat. "In fact, I think I have been really foolish, not considering anyone's feelings other than mine." Squeezing Snowball tightly, she added, "All right, we are going to New York tomorrow to see Jonathan Guyer, and we are going to have a wonderful time while we're there. Then when we return home, we'll go to see my Cherokee kinpeople. And we'll also have a good time with them. Now I've got to wash my face and go downstairs and find Joe and Celia." She set the cat down, and he immediately jumped back into the chair where he had been sleeping and began washing his face.

Mandie found her friends in the back parlor as they had promised. She was smiling when she entered the room and said, "This time tomorrow we'll be on our way to New York. I wonder what plans Jonathan Guyer has made for us." She sat down on a chair opposite them. Celia and Joe looked at each other.

"I hope he's not planning too many things. I'd like to see places that I didn't have time to visit when I was there before," Joe remarked.

"And my mother wants me to go shopping with her," Celia said.

"And I'm sure my mother will want us to go along with y'all," Mandie added.

"And I suppose Polly will want to tag along with y'all in the stores," Joe said with a big grin.

"Oh, I had almost forgotten about her," Mandie said, also grinning. "And her mother will probably give her lots of money to spend." Looking at Joe, she asked, "Are you not interested in shopping in New York?"

"Not really, but my father has said I should look for a nice overcoat," Joe replied. "And don't forget, my parents will both be going with us to visit your kinpeople when we return, Mandie. So I am supposed to buy something for a gift to your Uncle Wirt and Aunt Saphronia, and also Uncle Ned. So maybe you will be able to help me find something for them."

"Uncle John would probably be able to help you better than I could. Those are his kinpeople, too, and he knows them better than I do," Mandie said. She stood up and said, "Why don't we go for a walk before time to eat?"

"That's a good idea, Mandie," Celia agreed as she, too, rose.

"Looks like I'm outvoted, so I'll have to come along, too," Joe said, following the girls out of the room.

Outside they decided to go down to the rose arbor.

"Uncle John had all the debris removed from that old house that blew away in the tornado," Mandie remarked as they descended the hill.

"That was scary," Celia said, following Mandie. "I hope I never see a tornado again."

"That was the first tornado I've ever seen, and I hope I never see another one," Joe added, walking closely behind the girls.

"Look! There's someone down at the arbor," Mandie said, pointing ahead and quickening her step. Someone was sitting on the bench in the arbor.

"Yes, looks like a woman, doesn't it?" Celia agreed.

"You girls must have bad eyesight. That's your grandmother down there, Mandie," Joe said with a laugh.

Mandie stopped to stare ahead. "Oh, Joe, you're right," she agreed, walking faster. "I wonder what she's doing down there all by herself."

"She's sitting there enjoying this nice weather," Joe said teasingly.

As they approached, Mrs. Taft saw them coming.

"Well, Grandmother, we would have walked with you down here if we had known you were coming," Mandie said with a big smile, standing before the lady.

"Oh dear, Amanda, I can still find my way around this place," Mrs. Taft told her. "I just had to get away to think awhile."

The three young people sat down close by.

"Think, Grandmother? That sounds serious," Mandie said. "It must be something important."

Mrs. Taft looked at Mandie, smiled, and said, "Yes, indeed. You would think it is important."

"Mrs. Taft, can we help you with whatever it is?" Celia asked with concern in her voice.

"No, and before I am literally covered with questions, let me ask you one, Amanda. Why was it so important to you to go visit your kinpeople, which would have caused everyone else to change their plans?" Mrs. Taft asked.

Mandie took a deep breath, stared away down the hill, and finally turned to her grandmother. "You might not know this, but Uncle Ned brought that quilt back today that we had found in the attic during Christmas. Remember the one he said had a Cherokee message on it?" she asked, hoping her grandmother did remember the quilt.

Mrs. Taft frowned and said, "Yes, I remember seeing that quilt and that he took it home with him to have someone interpret the symbols on it." Then, looking sharply at Mandie, she asked, "Just what was the message?"

"That's the problem, Grandmother," Mandie began explaining. "Uncle Ned would only say that Uncle Wirt had looked at it and said to pack it away, it has a sad, bad message. And Uncle Ned absolutely refused to tell me what it did say, so I wanted to visit my Cherokee kinpeople and ask them what it says."

"But why the rush? Uncle Ned has had it since Christmas," her grandmother said.

"Well, Grandmother, Uncle Ned made such a mystery of it, I just wanted to go find out what it was all about," Mandie said and added, "And since Uncle Ned is here, I wanted to go home with him. He might not be here when we come back from New York, and I can't go see my kinpeople by myself. Then I realized I was being selfish to ask other people to change their plans for me."

"Young lady, you might be interested in knowing that I went to your mother for you, not knowing why, only that Elizabeth was upset because you insisted on changing everyone's plans. However, I figured you must have a good reason to want to do this," Mrs. Taft said.

"Oh, Grandmother, thank you," Mandie said with a big smile as she sat down on the opposite bench with her friends. "I hope Mother didn't get angry with you about it."

"Angry? No, she didn't. However, she refused to discuss it at all," Mrs. Taft replied. "I told her I didn't see any big reason for not changing our plans."

"I appreciate your trying, Grandmother," Mandie said. She glanced up and saw Liza hurrying down the hill. "Here comes Liza so fast she must have a message for one of us."

Everyone looked up as the girl got down to them. She was out of breath from her fast walking as she said, "Miz Lizbeth, she wants to see you, Missy 'Manda."

"Mother wants to see me?" Mandie repeated. "I wonder what for." She looked at her grandmother and asked, "Do you think I'm in trouble?"

Mrs. Taft smiled and said, "If you are and it's about our plans, just come let me know. I'll see what I can do to help you out."

"C'mon, Missy 'Manda," Liza insisted.

"Liza, take time to get your breath," Mandie told her as she stood up. "We'll just walk back up that hill. We won't run." Turning to her friends, she asked, "Are y'all going to wait down here?"

"Sure, we'll just stay here with your grandmother," Joe said. "Far away enough that we won't hear you scream for help."

"I'll wait here," Celia said.

"I'll remember that next time you get in trouble, Joe Woodard," Mandie said with a grin as she started up the hill with the maid.

Elizabeth was waiting for Mandie in the back parlor. There was no one else in the room. Mandie felt cold chills, wondering if her mother was angry with her about something. She tried to smile and didn't do a good job of it.

"Sit down, Amanda," Elizabeth told her as Liza left the room.

Mandie sat on a low stool, not too close to her mother, as she waited.

"Amanda, I don't know exactly how to say this," her mother began and then paused, looking around the room.

Mandie held her breath as she silently asked herself, *What have I done now?*

Elizabeth cleared her throat and said, "It seems that I am the only one who is opposed to changing our travel plans." Then she spoke quickly, "It might interest you to know that my mother was the one who started the revolt, so to speak, in your favor. Therefore, you may go home with Uncle Ned tomorrow morning and—"

"Oh, thank you, Mother," Mandie quickly interrupted.

"Wait, Amanda," Elizabeth told her. "I am not finished. If you and your friends wish to go home with Uncle Ned, you may. However, we adults will keep our plans and go on to New York tomorrow."

Mandie thought quickly for a moment. She would not be able to visit Jonathan Guyer if the others went on to New York without her. And then she remembered Polly. What would she do? "Mother, what about Polly? Will she still go with y'all or with us?" Mandie asked.

"I've talked to her mother, and she prefers that Polly go with us," Elizabeth replied.

"Oh," Mandie said in a loud whisper. She didn't like the idea of Polly Cornwallis going to visit Jonathan Guyer without Mandie and her friends along, too.

"You go talk to your friends and let me know what you plan to do," Elizabeth said.

"But, Mother, we wouldn't have to stay a long time with my kinpeople. Couldn't we come on to New York after we visit them for a few days?" Mandie asked.

"No, you young people certainly can't come all the way to New York without an adult along," Elizabeth said firmly.

Mandie stood up and said, "I'll go ask Celia and Joe what they would like to do."

"Go ahead and come straight back and let me know. We've got to settle this thing once and for all," Elizabeth said.

"Yes, ma'am," Mandie said, rushing out of the room.

She hurried outside and down the hill to where her friends were waiting. She did not follow her own advice to Liza not to hurry, and when she was half-way down, her foot slipped, causing her to sit down hard on a mound of dirt.

"Mandie!" Joe shouted as he ran up the hill to her. "Are you hurt?" He reached to help her stand up as Celia joined him, and back in the arbor, Mrs. Taft stood up to watch.

"No, only my pride," Mandie said as she brushed the dirt off her long skirts. "Come on. I have something to tell you, and I want Grandmother to hear it." She started on down toward the arbor.

"Amanda, that was very unladylike to come rushing down that hill in that fashion," Mrs. Taft reprimanded her.

"Yes, ma'am, I'm sorry, but you should hear what Mother wanted to see me about," Mandie replied, and she told them about the change in plans. She looked at Celia and Joe and said, "So if y'all want to go with me to visit my Cherokee kin-people, you can. Or y'all can go on to New York with the others."

"Couldn't we visit them for a few days and then go on to New York?" Joe asked.

Mandie shook her head as she said, "No, my mother said we could not come to New York alone, without an adult."

Mrs. Taft quickly spoke, "Amanda, I'm not in any particular hurry to go to Lindall Guyer's house. I could stay here and visit with friends for a few days while y'all go visit those kinpeople. Then we could all go to New York together. What do you think?" She smiled at Mandie.

Mandie rushed to embrace her and said, "Oh, Grandmother, I love you. You would do that for us?"

Mrs. Taft stepped away from the embrace and said, "Now that's settled. Once and for all, I hope. We will go speak to your mother."

"Thank you, Mrs. Taft," Celia said.

"I appreciate it, Mrs. Taft," Joe added.

"Come on. Let's hurry and talk to Mother," Mandie said, turning to go back up the hill.

"Not so fast this time, Amanda," Mrs. Taft reminded her.

"Yes, ma'am, Grandmother," Mandie said, slowing down and smiling at her.

Mandie could barely wait to settle the matter with her mother and then find Uncle Ned to let him know they would be going home with him. However, she planned to put the quilt in a bag so he wouldn't know that she was bringing it with her. Or he might even refuse to let her carry it, since he had been so firm about refusing to explain the message on the quilt.

But once among her kinpeople, Mandie was sure she would be able to find someone who would decipher the symbols for her.

Chapter 3 / A Disappearance

Elizabeth Shaw was still in the back parlor, but Jane Hamilton, Celia's mother, had joined her when Mandie and her friends and her grandmother came back to the house. Then Mandie realized Celia would have to get permission from her mother to change their plans.

Mandie whispered to Celia as they entered the room, "You have to get permission from your mother, remember?"

Celia nodded and went to sit near her mother. Joe and Mrs. Taft joined Mandie on a settee. "Mother, do you know about the change in our plans?" Celia asked.

Jane smiled at her and replied, "Of course I do, Celia. That's all we've been talking about today, this visit to see Amanda's Cherokee kinpeople and the journey to New York. So I suppose you want to go with Amanda?"

"Yes, ma'am," Celia replied with a big smile. "Please."

Mrs. Taft spoke up, "I have told the young ones I would wait here and visit friends while they go to see those kinpeople, and when they return I will accompany them to New York."

"Then that's fine, Celia. You may go with Amanda, but you do need to come on to New York when you get back because we have to do some shopping," Jane reminded her daughter.

"Mother, are you sure you don't want to go with us tomorrow?" Elizabeth asked, frowning as she looked at Mrs. Taft.

"As you very well know, I am not overly fond of visiting at Lindall Guyer's house, and this will cut my visit short," Mrs. Taft replied.

Mandie heard that remark and quickly looked at her friends, who were also looking at her. So her mother knew why her grandmother didn't like Mr. Guyer. But she was sure her mother would never tell.

"I know you don't like that enormous mansion with servants running all over the place, but Mr. Guyer does make us welcome so we don't have to stay in a hotel when we go to New York. And he does entertain us, so I just don't know why you've always disliked visiting there," Elizabeth said, frowning as she looked at her mother.

Mandie quickly absorbed that information. So maybe her mother did not know why Mrs. Taft seemed reluctant to go to Mr. Guyer's house. She looked at her friends again, and Joe and Celia were both frowning and shaking their heads, out of view of the adults.

Mrs. Taft didn't reply but rose and said, "I must go to my room now and rest a little before supper, now that we've got all these plans settled."

"Yes, Mother, thank you for altering your plans so eventually we will all be in New York together," Elizabeth said.

Mrs. Taft sent a secretive glance toward Mandie as she replied, "We'll let you know, Elizabeth, when to expect us in New York."

As soon as Mrs. Taft left the room, Elizabeth said, "Now, it's not all completely settled. Amanda, go find Uncle Ned and ask if you all may go with him in the morning. I believe he's out in the shed with your uncle John, tinkering around with something or other."

"Yes, ma'am." Mandie quickly stood up as she replied. "Come on, Celia, Joe, let's go."

They found Uncle Ned in the shed helping John Shaw mend a harness. As soon as they walked inside, Mandie began talking. "Uncle Ned, Mother and Celia's mother have agreed for us and Joe to go home with you tomorrow so I can visit my kinpeople. We just wanted to ask if we may go with you."

Before Uncle Ned could answer, John Shaw looked up from his work and said, "Now, this takes a little explaining. Are you all not going to New York?"

Mandie began relating the events of the day and ended by saying, "So you see, everything has been worked out just fine except that we need Uncle Ned's permission to go with him." She looked up at the tall Cherokee man.

Uncle Ned smiled at her and said, "We go, tomorrow sun come up, we go."

"Oh, thank you, Uncle Ned," Mandie said.

"And I thank you, Uncle Ned," Joe added.

"Yes, Uncle Ned, we appreciate your letting us go with you," Celia said.

"There's one problem," John Shaw spoke up.

"Oh no, what?" Mandie asked. She looked at her friends, who were both holding their breath.

"Uncle Ned is going over to Red Clay, Tennessee, to visit some friends a couple of days after he gets home and will not be able to come back with you all," John Shaw explained.

"Oh, shucks!" Mandie exclaimed.

"Will send another with Papoose and friends. We find someone, no worry," the old man said. Turning to John Shaw, he added, "No worry."

"Thank you, Uncle Ned," John Shaw replied, and turning to the young people, he said, "Remember this. You are not to start back home unless Uncle Ned has designated someone to travel with you. Remember that."

"Yes, sir," the three chorused.

"I have to go sort out my clothes now and pack," Mandie said.

"So do I," Celia added.

"Mine are all done. Remember, I put them in two piles?" Joe said. "I'll just stay out here while you girls pack."

Up in Mandie's room, the girls repacked their clothes. Mandie had two large valises and loaned one to Celia.

"We sure won't be needing a lot of clothes for this journey," Mandie told her. "One of these should hold everything necessary."

"Thank you," Celia said, taking the bag. "This won't take long to fill, either."

"I think I'd better unpack my trunk and hang all those clothes back up in the wardrobe, because by the time we come back here they will be all wrinkled," Mandie said, stooping to pull out dresses from her trunk.

Celia laughed and said, "We sure have been packing and unpacking, haven't we?"

"Yes, and I hope our plans are final now," Mandie agreed, taking the dresses to hang up in the wardrobe.

As soon as Celia had filled the valise, she said, "I'd better hang my other things back up, too, so they won't have to be pressed."

Finally everything was sorted, hung back up and packed into the valises. The girls looked around the room. Their empty trunks stood over to one side. Snowball had left the room as soon as they came in.

"I believe we're finished," Mandie said, and then she happened to look at the bed. "The quilt! Where is the quilt? Remember I left it on the bed when Uncle Ned gave it back to me? Oh, where is it?" She became excited as she quickly searched the room.

Celia helped look for it. "Yes, I remember it was on your bed," she agreed.

Mandie finished the search and stood in the middle of the floor as she said, "Oh, what happened to it? Celia, do you think Uncle Ned might have come in here and taken it back to hide somewhere since I didn't pack it away like he told me?"

"I don't think he would do that," Celia said, also puzzled.

"Somebody had to take it, because I am positive I left it on my bed," Mandie declared, stomping her foot. "And who would do that?"

"What are you going to do?" Celia asked.

"Oh, Celia, if I don't find that quilt, all this change of plans was for nothing," Mandie moaned.

"We'll just have to keep on looking for it," Celia replied.

"I just don't know where to start to look for it. It's not in this room. We both know that," Mandie said. She thought for a moment and then added, "I suppose we'll have to search all the bedrooms on this floor. I don't know what else to do." She started toward the door. "Come on. I know Joe didn't take it, but we need to search his room while he's down at the barn just in case someone put it in there while we were out."

"Search Joe's room? Suppose he catches us?" Celia said, following her out the door.

"We can just explain what we're doing," Mandie replied.

When they pushed open the door to Joe's room, Mandie noticed that Joe had sorted his clothes. There was one huge pile in each of the two chairs. His empty valise stood by the door.

"Let's hurry," Celia nervously whispered.

"Yes, we have lots of other rooms to do," Mandie agreed.

They searched the huge wardrobe and found it empty. The bureau drawers were also empty except for a few handkerchiefs. Mandie even got down on her knees and looked under the big bed. There was nothing under it, not even dust. The servants had cleaned the unused bedrooms that morning, knowing that guests would be arriving.

The Shaw house was three stories tall with an attic at the top. Aunt Lou, the housekeeper, and Liza, the maid, had rooms on the third floor. Jenny, the cook, and her husband, Abraham, the handyman, had their own cottage on the back of the property. Mr. Jason Bond, the caretaker, had a room near John Shaw's office, which was on the second floor.

Mandie and Celia quickly went through each room without being caught. Mrs. Taft was in her room, so they had to skip that one. They went back to Mandie's room and tried to figure out what to do next.

"The quilt has just disappeared," Mandie

declared. "Someone had to take it."

"It must be about time for supper, Mandie," Celia reminded her. "Let's go downstairs and see if Joe has come back into the house."

"Yes, he might have some ideas," Mandie agreed.

Joe came down the hallway just as they got to the bottom of the staircase.

"All done packing?" he asked.

"Yes, but, Joe, we have a problem," Mandie told him in a low voice. "Come on. Let's go to the back parlor, where we can talk a minute."

The back parlor was empty, and they went inside. Mandie closed the door. Before she even sat down she said, "Joe, the quilt is gone. I can't find it anywhere."

"The quilt is gone?" Joe asked as he sat on a settee. "If it's gone, someone had to take it. But who do you think would have done that?"

"I can't figure that out, Joe, unless Uncle Ned took it because I didn't pack it away like he told me to," Mandie replied, sitting on a nearby chair. "I had left it on my bed."

Celia sat down on a stool and said, "I told Mandie I don't think Uncle Ned would do that."

"I agree," Joe said. "But who would want to take the quilt? Are you sure one of the servants didn't just put it away in a cupboard or somewhere? Maybe thinking it didn't belong on your bed?"

"Maybe, but which one would do that? They're all busy in the kitchen getting food prepared. They cleaned the upstairs bedrooms this morning and would have no reason to go back up there that I know of," Mandie said. "If we can't find the quilt, there is no reason to go rushing off with Uncle Ned tomorrow morning." She got up to pace the floor. "Oh, who would do something like this?"

"We could start asking everyone if they have seen it," Celia suggested.

"But if we ask everyone about it, the person who took it would know we have missed it already and might just hide it in another place, wherever it is right now," Mandie said.

"Are you sure you're making sense, Mandie?" Joe teased.

"Well, what I meant was, I think it would be better if we don't tell everyone but just keep on looking for it," Mandie replied. "We've already searched all the bedrooms on the second floor except Grandmother's room. She is taking a nap, and we didn't want to disturb her. But as you know, there are lots of other rooms in this house, the third floor, and the attic, and all the downstairs."

"Mandie, I wish you would move into a smaller house. When we go on one of these searches, there's quite a bit of territory to cover in this house," Joe teased. "And I can remember doing it before, several times, in fact."

"But if we had a smaller house, we wouldn't have all those guest rooms for company to come and stay," Mandie reminded him. "And another thing about this quilt—I don't want my mother or anyone to figure out that that is the reason we're going home with Uncle Ned, because Uncle Ned might refuse to take us with him."

"Then we'd better get busy and search for this quilt," Joe told her.

At that moment Liza opened the door and stuck her head in to say, "Miz Lizbeth says be in de parlor in ten minutes. Supper gittin' ready."

"Thanks, Liza," Mandie told her as the girl

closed the door and went on down the hallway.

"I suppose we'd better get washed up and go to the parlor," Mandie told her friends. "We'll meet you in the main parlor in five minutes."

"I'll be there," Joe agreed.

Mandie and Celia hurried up to Mandie's room to wash up and comb their hair. As Mandie opened the half-closed door, she saw Snowball curled up asleep on her bed. "Just look at him, fast asleep. He doesn't know there's food ready downstairs," she said.

"Too bad he can't talk and tell you who came into your room and took the quilt," Celia said, going over to the bureau to get her comb and brush.

"If he was in here when they took it," Mandie said. "I know he has been in and out several times today. I'll just let him sleep and come back and get him for his supper if he doesn't come downstairs by the time we're finished with ours."

The girls hurried and were back downstairs in about five minutes. Everyone else was already in the parlor. They went to sit by Joe on a settee.

"You need to get to bed early tonight, Amanda," her mother reminded her. "You'll have to be up about daylight to get ready to go with Uncle Ned."

"Yes, ma'am," Mandie agreed.

"Yes, ma'am, me, too," Celia added.

"And I suppose that includes me, too," Joe teased.

"Mother, will you please tell Jonathan we'll be up later, that we didn't just forget about him inviting us to his house?" Mandie said.

"Of course, dear, but it would have been so much simpler for you three to just go along with us to New York and then visit your kinpeople after we get back, as we had planned," Elizabeth reminded her.

Mrs. Taft spoke up, "Now, Elizabeth, we've got that all settled. Let's don't cause another change of plans, please."

"I was just thinking," John Shaw said. "The way we had it planned was that we would all go to New York first and then go to visit our Cherokee kinpeople, but if you three are going to visit them first and we go on to New York and you all come on up there, I suppose we adults will be left out of any visit to our people."

Mandie smiled at him and said, "But we can go visit them again after we all come back from New York if y'all want to go then."

"Perhaps," John Shaw said. "We'll see."

By the time everyone was seated in the dining room for supper, Liza announced that Snowball was in the kitchen having his supper, too.

"Dat white cat, he eatin' in de kitchen," Liza said as she poured coffee for Mandie.

"That's fine, because now I won't have to go get him," Mandie said.

"Don't never have to git dat cat when he can smell food," Liza said, moving on around the table as she filled coffee cups.

Celia's mother, Jane Hamilton, spoke from across the table to her. "Celia, be sure you take enough warm clothes. It's still cold out there in the country hills. In fact, y'all might want to even take a quilt in the wagon with you for cover while you ride."

"Quilt?" Mandie said, almost choking on her food. Why had Mrs. Hamilton mentioned taking a quilt? Did she know about the missing quilt?

"Keep quilts in wagon," Uncle Ned said, over-hearing the remark. "No need more."

"That's nice, Uncle Ned," Jane Hamilton told him. "I suppose we're just not used to traveling much except on trains."

Mandie listened to the conversation, glanced at her friends, who were also listening, and decided it did not concern the missing quilt.

When the meal was over, Mandie and Celia decided to go up to Mandie's room and try to figure out what they could do about the quilt. Joe promised to meet them at the bench at the top of the main staircase as soon as he went to his room and packed his valise for their journey.

The door to Mandie's room was partly open, and when she pushed it wide, she saw that Snowball had returned and was already curled up in the middle of the bed again.

"Oh, that cat. He's going to sleep so much he'll keep us awake all night prowling around the house," Mandie complained. She went to the bed to talk to him. "Snowball, wake up and walk around awhile," she said. He opened one blue eye to glance at her and then closed it. "Come on, Snowball, get up," Mandie insisted. She bent over to pick him up. As she did, his claws stuck into the counterpane and dragged it with him.

Celia, who was standing nearby watching, started saying excitedly, "Mandie! Look! Look!"

Mandie stopped in surprise and looked at where Celia was pointing. The crumpled bedspread had revealed a quilt beneath it, and it was the Cherokee quilt. She quickly dropped Snowball on the floor and yanked the bedspread the rest of the way off the bed. Sure enough, it was the Cherokee quilt.

"Of all things!" Mandie said in surprise as she

knelt by the bed and crumpled up in laughter. "It was here all the time. I wonder who put it on the bed."

"That was a strange thing for someone to do, put that old quilt on the bed and then cover it with the bedspread," Celia said, excitedly looking at it.

"But who did it?" Mandie asked again.

"Thank goodness you found it, just in time, too," Celia reminded her.

Mandie stood up and said, "Will you help me take it off and fold it?"

The two girls finally got the heavy quilt off and folded.

"Now let's go tell Joe. He ought to be at the bench by now," Mandie said as they placed the quilt on a chair.

Celia said, "Wait, Mandie. I don't think we ought to leave that quilt out where someone might see it after all the trouble it has caused."

"You're right," Mandie agreed and looked around the room. "But where can I put it?"

At that moment there was a knock on the door, and Celia reached to open it. Liza was standing there. She was holding a clean sandbox for Snowball.

"Come in, Liza," Mandie said.

"I sees you all done found dat quilt," Liza said, glancing at the folded quilt on the chair. She set the sandbox in a corner.

"Yes. You don't know who put it on my bed, do you?" Mandie asked.

"I did dat, Missy 'Manda," Liza answered.

"You put it on my bed? But why?" Mandie asked.

"To hide it, Missy 'Manda," Liza replied. "I heard dat Injun man talking, dat quilt's got a secret, and he says to you to pack it away and you jes' go off and leave it right there where everybody could see it. So when I come to check all de rooms, I saw it and I hid it. Good hidin' place, ain't it?"

Celia and Mandie doubled up in laughter. Liza looked puzzled.

"Is there sumpin' funny?" Liza asked, puzzled by their behavior.

Mandie took a deep breath and said, "No, not really, Liza, but you see, we've been looking everywhere for this quilt." Then, as the girl still looked puzzled, Mandie added, "I'm glad you hid it for me. Otherwise someone might have taken it."

"Dat's right," Liza said. "Now I'se got to go."

"Good night, Liza. We'll see you bright and early in the morning," Mandie told her as the girl went on down the hallway.

"Well, that was a funny solution to that mystery. Come on, let's tell Joe," Mandie said, going to the door.

Celia asked again, "Are you not going to put it away, out of sight?"

Mandie paused and looked back. Snowball had crawled up on top of the quilt and was already fast asleep.

"Snowball will guard it for us. We'll only be gone a minute, and we will be able to see my doorway from that bench," Mandie told her.

When they told Joe about finding the quilt, he said, "I would say y'all had better get back to that room right now and lock the door to keep it from disappearing again. I don't want to have to stay up all night looking for it."

"You're right," Mandie agreed. "We'll see you around six o'clock in the kitchen tomorrow morning. Good night."

When they got back to Mandie's room this time, Mandie took another valise stored on top of the wardrobe and put the quilt in it. She set the valise right by the bed on the side where she would be sleeping.

"There, now. If anyone takes it, I'll be sure to wake," Mandie said, looking at the valise.

"Maybe we should lock the door," Celia suggested.

"Yes, that would be better," Mandie said, crossing to the door and turning the latch. "All safe and sound and ready to travel tomorrow."

She lay awake later that night, thinking about the quilt and wondering what kind of a message could be on it. She was so sure she would soon find out from one of her Cherokee kinpeople.

Chapter 4 / Mystery at Uncle Ned's

After taking several breaks along their way over the mountain with Uncle Ned the next day, the three young people and Snowball finally arrived with him at Deep Creek and went directly to his house, which was the largest one in the settlement. His wife, Morning Star, was in the yard.

"Welcome," the old woman greeted them as he stopped the wagon to let the young people out before Uncle Ned took it on to the barn for the night.

Mandie, holding on to her white cat, grabbed her valise and jumped down from the vehicle as Morning Star came forward to help them. Joe carried Mandie's extra valise containing the quilt.

Mandie reached to give the old woman a hug as she said, "Thank you, Morning Star. I hope you don't mind that we came earlier than we expected to." She knew Morning Star spoke very little English and probably didn't understand much, but the woman was always smiling and nodding her head in the affirmative when Mandie talked to her.

Morning Star turned to smile at Joe and Celia. Looking back at Mandie, she said, "Eat," and led the way into their house.

As soon as they stepped inside, Sallie, Uncle

Ned's granddaughter, who lived with him and Morning Star, came rushing down from upstairs and greeted them. "Mandie!" Sallie said in surprise. "I am so happy to see you all, Joe and Celia, too. I did not expect you all for two more weeks." She tossed back her long black hair.

"We only came to stay a few days. Mother and Uncle John and Mrs. Hamilton have gone on to New York," Mandie explained. "But Grandmother is waiting at home for us to come back so she can go with us to New York."

"Only a few days?" Sallie questioned her. "I had thought you would be staying a few weeks with us."

"Perhaps we can come back after we go to New York," Mandie told her. "We have our whole summer vacation ahead and plenty of time."

"Yes, please come back again after your journey to New York," Sallie said. "Come, we will take your bags upstairs." She led the way up to the attic rooms. "Joe, you will sleep over there," she added, indicating the small room on the other side of hers. "Mandie, Celia, you will sleep in here with me."

All this time Mandie was wondering what to do about the valise that contained the quilt. Should she take Sallie into her confidence?

"Here is your other valise, Mandie," Joe said, handing it over to her as he started toward the room he would use. Mandie stooped to set Snowball down.

"Thank you for carrying it for me, Joe," Mandie said, taking the bag from him and following Celia and Sallie into the room they would share. Snowball came along behind them and jumped up on one of the beds.

"Do you wish to hang up your clothes out of your bags?" Sallie asked, glancing at the two bags Mandie was carrying and the one Celia had.

"Some of them," Celia replied, taking a dress from her valise and hanging it up on a peg.

"Well, I suppose some of mine, too," Mandie said, deciding she would not tell Sallie about the quilt right now, maybe later. She set the valise containing the quilt in a corner and then pulled a dress out of the other one and hung it up beside Celia's.

"We will be going to visit Uncle Wirt and Aunt Saphronia tomorrow," Mandie told Sallie. The three girls sat on Sallie's bed.

"They were here last night," Sallie replied. "Their grandson has once again disappeared."

"Tsa'ni? Disappeared?" Mandie questioned. She called through the wall to the next room, "Joe, are you still there?"

"Yes, he has been gone since Friday of last week," Sallie replied.

Joe came to the doorway of the room and said, "But he has a habit of going off somewhere and not letting anyone know where."

"We will go downstairs now," Sallie said, rising from the bed. "My grandmother will be getting supper ready."

Mandie glanced at Snowball, who had curled up on the bed and was already asleep. "I hope he doesn't run off somewhere," she said to her friends.

"He has been here many times. I do not believe he will run away," Sallie said. "When he gets hungry, he will come down to the kitchen and we will feed him."

Mandie looked at the valise containing the quilt sitting in the corner and could not decide whether to mention the quilt to Sallie. After all, Uncle Ned was her grandfather, and Sallie might not approve of Mandie's insistence in finding out what the story of the quilt was. And she certainly didn't want to lose her friendship with Sallie. So Mandie went along with the others down to the huge kitchen, where the cooking food turned her thoughts to eating. They had brought their noon meal with them on the journey, but nothing could compare with Morning Star's cooking, unless it was the cooking of Aunt Lou, Uncle John's housekeeper.

Mandie sat next to Joe at the long table in Morning Star's kitchen, and she watched as he closely examined the food on his plate. She knew what he was doing, and she leaned close to him to whisper, "That is not owl stew. It's chicken." She grinned at him as he looked at her and blew out his breath.

"Thank you," he said. He picked up his fork and tasted of the meat. He smiled and nodded, "It's chicken."

Sallie, on the other side of Mandie, said, "We have chocolate cake left from our school picnic." She leaned to smile at Joe.

"Oh, thank you, that is the best part of the meal. I'll have to save room for a large piece," Joe said, grinning.

"Your school had a picnic?" Mandie asked.

"Yes, we had a picnic yesterday. Mr. Riley O'Neal has been able to persuade almost all of the Cherokee children to attend his school, and I have been helping a little with the teaching," Sallie explained.

"Oh, Sallie, I do hope you will become a teacher when you are grown," Mandie said between bites of stew. "You have the gift for it." Looking down the table to Celia, who was sitting on the other side of Joe, Mandie added, "Celia, you have been so quiet."

"I have been busy eating this wonderful food," Celia replied, leaning forward to smile at her friends. "We never have such good food at our school, do we?"

Mandie laughed and said, "No, it's always proper food and proper manners at the table, so I don't ever really enjoy it."

At that moment the schoolmaster of the school for the Cherokee children, Mr. Riley O'Neal, appeared at the open outside door and stepped into the kitchen. He smiled as he removed his large-brimmed hat and looked directly at Mandie. "Well, howdy, nice to see you all," he said, grinning at her.

"Oh, you are picking up the local language," Mandie said, laughing as she laid down her fork. He was from Boston and had an accent entirely different from that of the North Carolina people.

"Well, you know, since I'm one of the locals now, I thought I'd better begin talking like they do," he said, laughing.

Morning Star had jumped up from the table as soon as he had appeared and was setting a place for him across from the young people. "Sit, eat," she told him, smiling and pointing.

"But I was not expecting to eat with you," he told Morning Star as he sat down and she reached to pass the bowls of food.

Mandie knew he lived alone in a room built onto the Cherokee schoolhouse, and she imagined he was probably grateful for a meal at someone's house. He was a missionary, actually, with the title *Reverend*, who had come south to minister to the Cherokee children. He had also studied medicine and could take care of minor injuries or sickness at the Cherokee hospital that Mandie and her friends had built for the people with the gold they had found in the old cave. The Cherokee people had declared they would have nothing to do with the gold, that it had a curse on it, and insisted that Mandie take it. She had used it for their good.

"Eat," Morning Star insisted as she held the food out to him.

"Thank you, Morning Star," he said, taking large portions from the bowls she was passing.

"Tell me, Miss Amanda, when did you arrive?" Riley O'Neal asked as he finished filling his plate.

"Just a little while ago," Mandie replied.

"And will you be joining in the search for your cousin Tsa'ni Pindar?" the schoolmaster asked as he began devouring the food.

"Search for Tsa'ni? I didn't know people were concerned enough to begin a search for him. After all, he is always going off somewhere," Mandie replied. She took a sip of her coffee.

Uncle Ned spoke across the table, "Tsa'ni gone too long. Must be in trouble. We find," he said.

"Oh, if everyone is going on a search, of course I'll go with them," Mandie said.

"Grandfather of Tsa'ni worried about him," the old man explained. "Been looking, cannot find him. Wirt sent word, we search."

"He should learn to behave better," Joe said. "He just goes away on his own so often, people will finally quit looking for him because he always comes back."

"Yes, but remember that time we found him in a bear trap?" Mandie reminded Joe.

"One day he will grow up. Then we will stop worrying about him," Sallie said.

Looking across the table at Uncle Ned, Mandie asked, "When is this search supposed to begin?"

"Now," the old man replied. "We eat, then search, before dark."

Mandie glanced at her friends and asked, "All

right, I suppose we'll join in?''

They all agreed. Mandie was secretly disappointed to have to spend her time doing such a thing. She was anxious to find out about the quilt, and once she had done that she was in a hurry to return home and go to New York. Tsa'ni was her Cherokee cousin, but she knew he hated all white people. And that caused her to not want to help him in all his troubles and escapades.

Mandie looked up from her plate to see Dimar Walkingstick standing in the doorway smiling at her. He was not a relative of hers but lived in the mountains between Bird-town and Deep Creek with his mother, Jerusha.

"Dimar," Mandie said with a big smile as the boy entered the room. "I'm so glad to see you."

Everyone else turned to greet the boy. He was about the same age as Joe but not as tall. However, Mandie thought he was handsome.

"Sit, eat," Morning Star quickly said, jumping up once more to put another plate on the long table and motioning for the boy to sit.

"Your grandmother likes for everyone to eat," Dimar told Sallie as he sat on the other side of the long table.

Morning Star began filling his plate, not waiting to ask what he wanted to eat. She had learned long ago that this boy would eat anything she gave him.

"I suppose you have come to join in the search for Tsa'ni?" Riley O'Neal asked.

"Yes, his grandfather sent word," Dimar replied, picking up his fork and beginning to eat the food before him. Looking at Mandie and her friends, he said, "I did not know you all were coming today."

Mandie explained their schedule to him. While she was doing this, she was secretly wondering if perhaps Dimar would translate the message on the Cherokee quilt for her. She knew he was always very friendly with her. And, too, he was not a Cherokee relative. From what she had gathered, Uncle Ned had indicated that the whole Cherokee clan of kinpeople had refused to discuss the quilt. She might take Dimar into her confidence if she got a chance alone with him.

"I brought two lanterns," Dimar was telling Uncle Ned.

"So did I," Riley O'Neal added. "However, we have lots of daylight left yet today, so I am hoping we will find him before darkness falls."

"Where are we going?" Celia asked, looking at Dimar.

Dimar smiled at her and replied, "Up this side of the mountain and down the other side. Jessan, father of Tsa'ni, will meet us at top."

Mandie glanced at Celia and noticed that her friend did not seem very enthusiastic about this search. Celia was not used to country life in the Cherokee country. She lived on a huge plantation with her mother and her aunt just outside of Richmond, Virginia, and was in the social life there.

"Celia, if you don't want to go with us, you don't have to, you know," Mandie said.

Celia quickly replied, "But I want to if you are all going." And then, grinning at Mandie, she added, "I'm not afraid of darkness and mountains like Polly Cornwallis is."

Polly Cornwallis! That was another reason for Mandie to hurry home. The girl had gone with Mandie's and Celia's mothers and Uncle John to New York, and there was no telling what she would get involved in. Mandie could always depend on Polly to do unexpected things. Oh, she just had to find out what the message on the quilt was so she could get home and on to New York.

"Yes, Polly is afraid of her shadow," Mandie replied with a grin.

"And everyone else's shadow," Joe added, also grinning.

Also, Mandie was anxious to see her uncle Wirt Pindar and his wife, Saphronia. She would try to find out why Wirt refused to translate the message on the quilt without his knowing what she was doing.

At that moment Snowball came running into the kitchen, loudly purring and going to rub around Mandie's ankles.

Morning Star once again jumped up and said, "Eat," as she took a plate from the shelf by the dry sink.

Everyone laughed. The old woman always wanted everyone to eat, even the cat. And Snowball, sensing where the food was, immediately went to rub around Morning Star's ankles as she filled the plate for him.

"Eat," everyone chimed in as Morning Star set the plate down by the stove for the white cat.

Finally everyone rose from the table, and Sallie said, "We must get coats. It will be cold later tonight."

She led the young people upstairs, where Mandie and Celia took out coats from their luggage. Sallie took hers from a peg, where it was hanging. Dimar had walked upstairs with Joe, saying, "I have my coat on my horse."

"I'll get mine," Joe told him.

As the girls were leaving the bedroom upstairs, prepared with their coats, Mandie glanced back and was shocked to see that the extra valise containing the quilt was no longer in the corner. She quickly stepped back and looked around the room. There was no sign of it.

Sallie and Celia were going out the door, and Mandie had to follow them.

"Maybe this will not take long," Sallie was saying. "Perhaps we will find Tsa'ni soon and we may not need the coats."

Joe and Dimar were leaving the other room and followed the girls downstairs. Mandie kept trying to get Joe's attention, but he was busy talking to Dimar. She looked at Celia, and she was busy talking to Sallie.

Oh, what was she going to do? Someone had taken the quilt, and Mandie couldn't even let Uncle Ned and Sallie know that she had brought it with her. How would she ever find it when the only ones she could mention it to were Celia and Joe?

Mandie frowned and stomped her feet as she went down the steps into the yard behind the others. Well, someone must have known she had brought it, but who? She didn't believe Uncle Ned had been upstairs since they came, and not only that, she didn't think he would do such a thing.

Then there were Riley O'Neal, who had probably never heard of the quilt, and Dimar, who had come in the kitchen and stayed there while they ate.

But someone had taken the quilt. And how was Mandie ever going to get it back?

Chapter 5 / Up the Mountain

Everyone gathered in Uncle Ned's yard, preparing to begin the search. Mandie couldn't keep her mind on their plans as she thought about the missing quilt. She had brought a cloak with her from home, and she pulled the hood up over her blond hair as the evening chill settled over them. Everyone seemed to be talking at once, and she was not paying attention to what they were saying.

"Dimar is getting Uncle Ned's cart for us to ride in up the mountain, and then at some point we'll get out and walk where the bushes are too thick and there is no trail," Joe was explaining to her.

Mandie blinked her eyes and whispered, "Joe, the quilt is gone. I left it in the valise in Sallie's room, and when I went back to the room just now it had disappeared. What will I do?"

Joe looked concerned as he replied, "I suppose nothing right now. We are expected to go on this search since everyone is going. We'll look for it when we get back." Then he added loudly, "Here is Dimar now."

Dimar drove the cart into the front yard, and Sallie beckoned to them. "Come on. We will ride in the cart for a while," she said, walking over to the vehicle.

Mandie followed Sallie, Celia, and Joe into the cart. They sat on the floor, which was covered with several blankets. She quickly looked around, but there was no quilt in the vehicle. She would be looking at and searching everything until she found the old quilt. She had thought maybe someone had taken it for cover in the cart, but even that idea didn't make sense. Why would anyone take it out of her valise and put it in the cart? And what would they have done with the empty valise, anyhow?

"I'll ride alongside the cart with you," Riley O'Neal was telling Dimar as Mandie settled her long skirts and looked at the adults who were all mounting horses, even Morning Star, who rode astride and could keep up with any of the men. Mandie noticed two young Indian braves who had evidently just joined the party.

Uncle Ned straightened up in his saddle and gave instructions. "We go to mountain. We take east side, young ones in cart take west side. We meet at top. We shoot gun to sky two times if we find Tsa'ni."

"Where do we meet Mr. Wirt and the others?" Riley O'Neal asked, trying to steady his horse.

"Wirt lead search up north side. We on south side now," the old Indian explained. "Who get to top first must wait. Go now." He shook the reins and led the way out of his yard.

Mandie had been out with search parties before, and she knew how thorough the Indian people were. They wouldn't miss a single thing, not even a broken twig left to mark the trail. Dimar drove slowly because the road to the mountains was bumpy. There was not much conversation among the young people until they finally arrived at the base of the mountain and everyone got out, prepared to climb the mountain trail ahead of them.

The three girls raised their skirts and jumped down from the cart as Joe tried to assist all of them at once.

Riley O'Neal dismounted and tied his reins to a bush while Dimar tethered the horse pulling the cart.

"We must walk now, and we must take the lanterns and guns with us," Dimar explained as he reached for two guns from under the seat of the cart. Turning to Joe, he handed him one and said, "This is for you."

"I can carry a lantern, Dimar," Mandie said.

"And I will carry one, too," Sallie added.

"Since there are only two lanterns, what will I carry?" Celia asked, looking around the floor of the cart.

"Here, the bag with supplies for injuries," Dimar said, handing her a small cloth bag.

"And I have another supply bag," Riley said as he walked over to join them. "Only mine is full of food." He held his lantern, slung the bag over his arm, and then balanced his gun on shoulder. He looked directly at Mandie and smiled.

Mandie, catching his eye, felt herself blush for some reason, and she quickly stepped over to join Sallie and Celia, who were already following Dimar toward the trail. Joe was checking the ammunition in the rifle Dimar had given him and he hurried forward to join them, leaving Riley O'Neal to bring up the rear. Uncle Ned and the others had gone in the opposite direction.

Mandie was deep in thought about the missing quilt when they began to ascend the mountain and she suddenly heard a very loud *meow* behind her.

Stopping to turn around, she yelled, "Snowball, where did you come from?"

Everyone else paused as they turned back to look. There was the white cat daintily picking his way through the brush toward his mistress.

"He must have been walking behind us all the time. We weren't riding very fast," Mandie said with a loud moan as she waited for Snowball to catch up.

"I'll carry him for you, Mandie. I only have this little bag and you have the lantern," Celia offered, stooping to catch the white cat as he passed her. She put him on her shoulder as she had seen Mandie do.

"Thank you, Celia, but I'll take him now and then. You'll get too tired, because he is heavy," Mandie said.

"And I will help carry him," Sallie added.

"I don't think I want to carry that white cat, because he gets excited and scratches sometimes. But I will carry anything else anyone wants to get rid of," Joe said, looking around the group.

"So will I," Dimar said.

"That's a smart cat. He doesn't speak our language, but he certainly knew we were going away and leaving him behind, and he just decided to join us," Riley O'Neal teased Mandie.

"Oh yes, I'd even say Snowball is a mind reader," Mandie joked back. "He always seems to know when I am going somewhere. He's been on searches before with me in these mountains."

"We go now," Dimar called from the front of the line as he continued up the mountain.

Now and then Mandie noticed other young Cherokee men evidently searching the bushes along the way. Dimar always held up his hand in silent salute to them. So there must be quite a few people combing the mountain for Tsa'ni, who never seemed to care how much time and trouble he caused other people.

As they got deeper and deeper into the mountain, it grew darker and darker. Finally Dimar halted the group. "We rest five minutes and light our lanterns now," he told them as everyone gathered around a fallen log and sat down.

The light from the lanterns made eerie shadows through the trees, and Mandie shivered.

"Are you cold?" Joe asked, sitting next to her.

"Not really," she replied as the others stopped talking among themselves to listen. "I think it's fright, just thinking about all the wild animals who could be lurking out there in the dark." She shrugged her shoulders and pulled her cloak closer around her. Snowball, who had been allowed down, jumped up into her lap.

"Do not be afraid. We have guns," Dimar reminded her.

"Perhaps we will soon find Tsa'ni," Sallie said.

"Who last saw Tsa'ni?" Mandie asked. "What was he wearing? What color clothes are we looking for? No one has explained all this."

"He came by the house of my grandfather last Friday. He was wearing a tan shirt and breeches, something that will not be easy to see in the woods," Sallie explained. "Everyone thinks that is the last time anyone saw him."

"What did he have to say? Was he planning on going anywhere else?" Mandie asked.

"He did not talk at all. He came into the kitchen, and my grandmother gave him a cup of coffee. He sat on the back doorstep and drank it, and he disappeared while my grandmother was in the kitchen for a few minutes. No one saw him leave."

"That sounds about like him," Joe remarked. "He is always trying to seem mysterious and aloof from everyone else."

"He was at school that morning," Riley O'Neal added. "When everyone came back inside from recess at noon, he was no longer there."

"His grandfather Wirt said he had asked to go to Asheville with his father, Jessan, that morning, but his mother would not allow him," Dimar said. "Jessan was going for supplies and would not return until later this week."

"Did anyone see him between the time he left school at recess and when he came by Uncle Ned's house?" Celia asked. "Maybe he told someone else where he was going."

"Time up, we go," Dimar said, picking up one of the lighted lanterns and standing up.

"Now that it's dark, I will bring up the rear to be sure no one gets lost along the way," Riley O'Neal told the group, rising with his lantern, rifle, and bag.

As they slowly climbed the narrow trails up the mountain, Mandie tried to focus her mind on Tsa'ni, to figure out why he disappeared and where he had gone. She figured he was probably angry at not being allowed to go to Asheville with his father and had deliberately disappeared to cause worry among his people.

The group walked a long way up the mountain without seeing any of the other searchers. Dimar kept them at a slow pace because now that it was dark, the ones who had lanterns flashed their lights to either side as they went. Since the leaves were not fully out on the trees and bushes, it was possible to see quite a distance into the woods. Several deer scampered away from them, and now and then there were rustling sounds of other animals.

Mandie thought about New York, and then she suddenly realized that the plans for Joe's parents to come visit the Cherokee people with them were going to be ruined because Mandie and her friends had come here first. They were walking single file, and she was immediately in front of Joe. She turned back and said, "Joe, your father said he would bring your mother to my house when we came back from New York so they could come out here with us, remember?"

Joe scratched his head and said, "That's right." He thought for a moment and added, "Maybe my mother will want to go to New York with us."

"I'm sorry, but I forgot all about them," Mandie apologized.

Celia, walking ahead of Mandie, looked back to say, "Mandie, your mother might have sent word to Joe's parents that our plans had changed."

"I hope someone let them know," Mandie replied, and then she leaned forward and said in a low voice, "I'll be glad when we get done with this search. The quilt disappeared out of Sallie's room."

"What?" Celia exclaimed, slowing to look back. "How do you know?"

"When we went back to get our coats, it was gone," Mandie continued whispering. Snowball, on her shoulder, started meowing loudly, and she couldn't say any more.

Suddenly a shot rang out faintly through the woods. The entire group froze in their tracks to listen. After a couple minutes Dimar motioned to them. "Come on. That's not a signal for us. We arranged that if any of us needed help or found Tsa'ni we would fire twice. That was only one shot," he explained.

Mandie shifted Snowball to her other shoulder and moved on behind Celia. The cat was heavy, and she was tired. She wondered how much farther they had to go to reach the top and meet the others. In her opinion this was all a waste of time. Tsa'ni would show up whenever he got ready. He always did—most of the time, anyway. Maybe if the people would stop organizing search parties to look for him every time he decided to run off somewhere, he would quit disappearing. And why did the search have to be at night? Why couldn't they have waited until morning to do this?

Their group was the first to reach the top of the mountain. Dimar knew their plans as to where to wait. He led them to a large clearing where the moon was shining through the few trees there. Mandie could see several fallen logs and a stream nearby glistening from the moonlight.

Riley O'Neal stepped forward to set his bag on one of the logs. "We will have a bite to eat while we wait for the others," he told the group as he opened the bag and began withdrawing the contents.

"Yes, food," Joe agreed, watching to see what Riley had.

"We have ham biscuits and sausage biscuits," Riley announced, looking around the group.

"You made ham and sausage biscuits?" Mandie asked.

Riley grinned at her and said, "I only carried them. Morning Star made them today and gave them to me for our group. Everyone just step forward and take whatever you want." He stepped back from the stack of biscuits he had pulled out of the bag and laid on a cloth on the log.

Mandie had trouble controlling Snowball until she took a ham biscuit, sat down nearby, and broke off a piece for her cat. He greedily ate it and meowed for more.

"Snowball, you are not going to have my whole biscuit. You had your supper," Mandie told the cat as he rubbed against her ankles.

"There is plenty, Mandie," Sallie said. "Why not give him his own biscuit?"

"Yes, there is more than we will eat. After all, we did eat the huge supper that Morning Star cooked," Riley O'Neal said. Reaching for a ham biscuit, he held it out to the cat and then laid it on the grass for him. "Here, Snowball." He sat down next to Mandie on the log.

Snowball went to work on the biscuit. He didn't just pull out the meat and eat it. He ate the biscuit, too, as everyone watched.

Mandie looked at Riley and asked, "Is your school out now for the summer?"

"Not exactly," he replied. "We haven't been able to get the school on a regular schedule because there are so many holidays and other excuses for the Cherokee children not to come to school. They are not used to regular sessions like the white children are. I discussed this with your old schoolmaster, Mr. Tallant, at Charlie Gap the other day. He suggested having rewards for attendance. I may try that."

"Reward them for going to school?" Joe asked.

"Yes," Sallie spoke up. "Our children are not used to the ways of the white children. They can be enticed to do things if there is a reward for it."

"And most of the children are fast learners," Riley added.

Dimar suddenly stood up, waved his hand at everyone, and whispered, "Shhh!"

Everyone stopped talking to listen. Mandie could not hear a sound at first, but then she finally realized someone or something was walking through the woods nearby. Then it dawned on her that they were in plain view in the moonlight if this was danger of any kind. However, Dimar stood there and no one moved.

Then Snowball broke the silence. He meowed loudly and went running off in the direction of the sound.

Dimar laughed and said, "It's Uncle Ned and the others."

At that moment the old man appeared in the moonlight nearby, and Mandie saw Snowball rubbing around his ankles. He came forward to join them.

"Cat here, too," he said, laughing as he stooped to pat Snowball's head.

"Oh, I'm glad it was you, Uncle Ned," Mandie said, blowing out her breath. "Snowball could have caused us trouble."

"Where is the rest of your party, Uncle Ned?" Riley O'Neal asked.

"Over other side, wait for Wirt," he explained. "I come see you come."

"We have not seen anyone," Dimar told Uncle Ned. "If Tsa'ni is on this mountain, he is not on this side."

"Not other side, either," Uncle Ned replied. "Maybe Wirt find on his side. We see."

Uncle Wirt approached them from the woods then. He was alone. "Tsa'ni not there," he said as he stood before the group.

"Nowhere," Uncle Ned added.

Dimar stood before them and asked, "Now we go down long way?"

"Yes," Uncle Ned said.

Wirt nodded and said, "Long way."

Riley O'Neal quickly repacked what was left of the biscuits, and everyone got their things together. Mandie picked up Snowball.

Joe groaned and said in a whisper to Mandie, "The long way. It's probably twice as long as the way we came. We may be finished by daylight."

"Oh shucks!" Mandie exclaimed.

"The long way is really the short way," Sallie explained as they began following the old men. "Because we go down faster than we come up."

"That sounds good," Joe said.

"If we don't find Tsa'ni on this mountain, I wonder where we look next," Mandie said. "I'm going to tell him a thing or two when we do catch up with him." She held on to Snowball and followed her friends down a steep hill.

Chapter 6 / No Luck

Sallie was right. The way down took much less time than the way up had. At the bottom of the mountain, the young people piled into the cart again and followed the adults back to Uncle Ned's house. The night air had grown chilly, and as soon as the animals were all put away, everyone gathered around the huge fireplace in Morning Star's immense kitchen. She immediately began serving hot coffee, and Sallie brought out a blackberry pie that she had made earlier.

Finally everyone ended up at the long table. Snowball jumped into the woodbox behind the huge iron cookstove and curled up for a nap.

"I thought I'd want to go to bed as soon as I got back, but this food is worth staying awake for," Joe told Morning Star, who looked at Sallie for interpretation.

Sallie spoke in the Cherokee language to her grandmother, and Morning Star replied with a big smile.

"My grandmother says she enjoys feeding hungry people," Sallie told the young people.

"And we enjoy the food, Sallie," Celia said, taking a bite of the pie.

"Yes," Joe agreed.

"Everything she cooks is delicious, but I know you made the pie, Sallie, and you are also a good cook," Mandie said, sipping her coffee.

"Thank you," Sallie said shyly.

"Now, what do we do next?" Riley O'Neal asked Uncle Wirt.

The young people immediately grew quiet to listen.

Uncle Wirt shook his head and said, "Tomorrow we search woods, other way." The old man indicated the opposite direction from the mountain with his hand.

Dimar spoke up. "Tsa'ni may not want us to find him, and if that is so, we will never find him." He looked at the men.

"After woods, no more," Uncle Wirt replied. "Jessan be home soon. He find."

Mandie was relieved to hear that. She didn't want to spend all her time looking for the missing boy, but she knew from past experiences that when one is missing, all the rest in the area are expected to search. She was sitting between Joe and Celia and whispered, "We need to find the quilt." She quickly looked at Sallie on the other side of Celia, but Sallie didn't seem to hear her.

Mandie was still thinking about how she could get someone to tell her what the message on the Cherokee quilt was. She decided she would not even mention the quilt to Uncle Wirt. He could be loud and determined in his views about various things. And he had told Uncle Ned to bring the quilt back and to tell Mandie to put it away.

Suddenly Joe stood up and said, to everyone in general, "Excuse me for a minute. I need to get something from my luggage."

Mandie opened her mouth to ask what, but he ignored her and quickly left the room. She looked at Celia, puzzled by his behavior. Celia shrugged her shoulders to silently say she didn't know what was going on.

The adults talked on while Mandie, Celia, and Sallie silently waited for Joe to return. And when he came back into the room, he held something behind him and went directly to Morning Star.

"This is for you," he said, smiling as he brought forth a red silk scarf and quickly placed it around the old woman's neck.

Morning Star reached to squeeze his hand, jumped up from the table, and twirled around with the scarf flowing from her shoulders. "Pritty, pritty," she kept repeating.

Then Uncle Wirt and Uncle Ned nodded with big smiles and said, "Pritty, pritty," together.

Everyone laughed. Joe sat back down next to Mandie and said, under his breath, "Quilt not back."

Mandie frowned and sighed. "Where did you get the scarf?" she asked.

"I had it with me when I came to your house," Joe explained. "And it really was for Morning Star. My mother gave it to me to put in my valise for her to bring to Morning Star when we were all supposed to come here together later."

Mandie watched Morning Star, who was seated back at the table but kept running her fingers through the tassels on the ends of the scarf.

"The scarf is beautiful, Joe. My grandmother may never want to take it off again," Sallie said with a laugh.

Dimar leaned forward to ask, "Do all women like scarves?"

Mandie smiled at him and said, "Most women, I'd say."

"Then I must get one for my mother. She will see Morning Star's and will wish to have it," the Indian boy said.

Sallie looked at Dimar and said, "I do not know where you will find one."

"I will have to go to Bryson City and look for one," Dimar replied.

Riley O'Neal, sitting across the table, had been listening to the young people's conversation. "I will be going to Bryson City one day sometime within the next week. I would be glad to look for a scarf for you, Dimar."

"Thank you," Dimar said. "If you are going there, I would appreciate it."

"Yes, I am going there to look for a lady who makes quilts for sale," Riley O'Neal replied. "I have decided I need a little more cover for these cold winter nights. I know it's springtime, but I will be prepared for next winter."

Uncle Wirt had overheard this from down the table, and he looked at Riley and said, "No buy quilt. Saphronia have lots and lots quilts. She give you one."

"Thank you very much, Mr. Wirt. I would be glad to pay her for any extra quilt she may be able to spare," Riley said.

Mandie had straightened up at the first word about quilts. She quickly debated whether to speak or not. She really wanted to see Aunt Saphronia's quilts, mainly to decide whether she had any that might have a Cherokee message on them like the one she had found.

"You help Cherokee children, no pay for quilt," Uncle Wirt told Riley.

Looking at Dimar, Riley said, "I still have to go to Bryson City for other things." Then to Wirt he said, "Thank you."

Mandie knew the Cherokee people didn't like to be paid for any gifts they might wish to give white people. And evidently Riley knew this, too.

"Tomorrow we look more," Uncle Wirt said, rising from the table. "Now we sleep."

Everyone stood up around the table.

"I will be going home now, too," Dimar told them. "I will return early tomorrow morning to help search."

"And so will I," Riley O'Neal added. "Since we don't have any schooling for this week, I'll be free to help in any way that I can."

Uncle Wirt looked at Mandie and smiled. "You will come see us after that," he said.

"Yes, sir, Uncle Wirt. I'll be over at your house as soon as we can finish this searching," Mandie promised, grinning at the man who was her father's uncle and brother to her deceased grandmother, Talitha Pindar Shaw.

Uncle Wirt turned to the other young people and said, "All come to my house then."

Joe, Celia, and Sallie replied together, "Yes, sir."

As everyone said good-night and the young people went upstairs to sleep, Mandie frowned at Joe and tried to catch his attention. "Look for the quilt," she whispered, dropping back beside him and letting Sallie and Celia go ahead.

Joe nodded.

With Sallie in the room with her and Celia, Mandie could not talk to Celia about the quilt. She had decided not to say a word to Sallie about it. Joe and Celia would be on the lookout for it.

Mandie lay awake for a long time after Celia and Sallie had gone to sleep. She tried and tried to figure out what had happened to the quilt. How would she ever find it?

Suddenly she heard horse's hooves in the yard below, slow and soft, as though someone was walking the animal. She quickly slid out her side of the bed and hurried over to the window to look out. The night was dark, and she couldn't see a thing down there. However, she believed whoever it was, was making sure they were outside the range of her vision. She debated going downstairs and out-side to investigate but decided against it. This was Uncle Ned's house, and he probably wouldn't like it if he caught her roaming around in the darkness.

Then she heard a board creak outside the bed-room door. Rushing over to throw her cloak around her shoulders, she opened the door softly and saw Joe creeping past, evidently headed for down-stairs.

Joe saw her and stopped and put his fingers to his lips to indicate no talking. Mandie nodded and motioned that she would wait there.

Mandie waited and waited, sitting on the floor outside the bedroom door, and was about to go down and find out where Joe had gone. Then with-out a sound Joe came back and motioned to her with his hands, "Gone. No one there." He went on to his room.

Mandie sighed and went back to bed. She finally went to sleep and dreamed someone was chasing her through a dark tunnel. She suddenly jerked awake as Sallie stood there, touching her shoulder.

"Time for breakfast," Sallie told her.

Mandie sat up and looked around. Celia was

also up and already dressed. "My goodness, I'm late. I'm sorry," she said. "I'll be ready to go downstairs in two minutes."

She threw back the covers, dislodged Snowball, who loudly protested, and hurried to put on her clothes.

"Did I hear someone with a horse come through the yard last night, or was I dreaming?" Mandie asked her friends, closely watching to see if they had heard the sound, too.

"I didn't hear anything. I slept soundly all night," Celia said.

"Yes, I heard someone, too," Sallie replied. "But that is not unusual lately, because my grandfather has young men watching all night around the house in case Tsa'ni comes through here."

"Well then, that must explain what I thought I heard," Mandie said, quickly brushing her long blond hair. As she turned with the hairbrush, she quickly looked into every corner of the room. There was still no sign of the missing valise with the quilt.

Joe joined the girls outside their doorway, and when the young people got downstairs, Morning Star had breakfast ready. Dimar and Uncle Wirt were already in the kitchen.

As Morning Star motioned for everyone to sit down at the table, Riley O'Neal came in through the back door and joined them. After rushing ahead of them downstairs, Snowball was sitting by the iron cookstove washing his face.

There was not much conversation during the meal, since everyone was in a hurry to get on with the search and get it over with.

Uncle Wirt explained how they were to split up

and cover the woods on the other side, away from the mountain.

Mandie didn't want to look after Snowball during this search. She asked Uncle Ned, "Will it be all right if I shut Snowball up in the bedroom upstairs while we are gone?"

"Yes, shut up cat," the old man agreed with a big smile, and then he turned to translate this to his wife.

Morning Star also smiled and said, "Cat up."

That was a great relief. Mandie would take him upstairs and leave him. Then she realized something else. "Oh, he will need a sandbox if he is left up there all day," she said.

"I will get a sandbox for Snowball," Dimar volunteered.

When everyone had finished the meal, Dimar went outside to prepare a sandbox for Snowball. The girls helped Morning Star clear the table and pack a large quantity of biscuits with ham and sausage for their noontime meal, wherever they were at that time.

"Make three," Uncle Wirt told Sallie. "We go three ways."

"Yes, sir," Sallie replied and found three flour sacks, which she filled with food.

Dimar came back inside with a wooden box full of sand. Mandie told him, "I'll get Snowball and take him upstairs now."

"Food," Morning Star insisted. "Food."

"Yes, food and water," Sallie said, going to the dry sink to fill a tin bowl with water from the buckets of water standing there.

"I'll get the food," Celia said, reaching down to pick up the bowl of food and causing Snowball to protest.

Mandie picked up the cat and said, "Don't worry, Snowball. We are only moving you upstairs. You can have your food back up there."

After finally settling her cat in Sallie's bedroom, Mandie waited to be the last one to leave the room so she could be sure the door was closed and Snowball could not get out.

"I suppose we are all ready now," Mandie remarked as she, Sallie, Dimar, and Celia returned to the kitchen.

Joe grinned at Mandie and said, "I'm glad you packed that cat away so we won't have to go on a search for him, too." He was holding the rifle Dimar had loaned him the day before.

"I'm beginning to believe it would be much easier to have to hunt for Snowball than it is to hunt for Tsa'ni," Mandie replied.

Outside in the early morning light, Mandie tried to see whether there were hoof prints in the yard but decided there would be some anyway from all the other horses coming in and out.

They split up into three parties, with Uncle Wirt directing them as to which way each group should go. The young people were all together again, with Riley O'Neal and Dimar to lead them. Several other young men had joined them in the yard and went with the other two parties.

Not having slept very much the night before, Mandie soon grew tired and seemed to be lagging behind everyone else after a couple of hours of walking and searching the bushes in the forest into which their route took them.

Riley O'Neal, bringing up the rear, said loudly to Dimar, who was in the lead, "I believe we should take a short break by that creek up ahead."

Dimar looked back, smiled, and said, "I agree."

Riley glanced at Mandie as she turned to look at him, and she smiled in gratitude.

As the group stopped by the creek and sat on fallen logs, Dimar suggested, "Why don't we eat a biscuit now? And then in another two hours we could eat another one and so on. That way we would not have to stay long in one place."

"Yes," was chorused by the young people.

As they ate, Mandie asked Dimar, "Do you think we will be searching all day? Or in other words, will this take the whole day just looking for Tsa'ni?"

"Most of the day," Dimar replied. "It depends on how fast we move along. And also whether the other two groups meet us at the planned place by the river when we get there. They may be slower. Or they could be faster."

Mandie sighed loudly. "I think Tsa'ni should be locked up or something so he can't run away and waste all our time," she said.

"Impossible to lock up Tsa'ni," Riley said. "He can get out of anything."

"Except the bear trap we found him in one time before," Joe added.

"When will his father return from Asheville?" Mandie asked.

"Any time now," Dimar said.

"I believe Tsa'ni followed his father to Asheville," Sallie said, finishing her ham biscuit.

"Then I hope his father punishes him good," Celia said.

"He will, but it doesn't do much good," Riley said, drinking water from a cup he had filled in the spring nearby.

"I still think if everyone just ignored him and did not go on these searches for him, he would quit running away so much," Mandie replied. "And we need to be thinking about that and figuring what can be done."

"Yes, his grandfather, Mr. Wirt, has been saying the same thing," Dimar said, rising to pick up his rifle. "Now we go on so maybe it will not take all day." He smiled at Mandie.

Mandie hoped it would not take all day. She had decided that after today's search she would drop out and go to visit her Cherokee kinpeople over at Bird-town.

Much later in the day the three groups met at the river. Nothing had been found that might even lead to Tsa'ni. Mandie listened as the adults discussed what they had been doing on these searches. She could tell that Uncle Ned was tired and losing interest in finding Tsa'ni.

"We go home now," the old man said. "No more search today."

Then Uncle Wirt surprised them all as he added, "No more search at all."

The young people sighed with relief.

"We go home now," Uncle Ned told the group. "Eat."

Even though Morning Star was with them again on this search, Mandie knew supper wouldn't take long to prepare. The old woman had left a stew cooking in the iron kettle hanging in the fireplace. And the thought of food gave Mandie another reason to want to get back to Uncle Ned's house.

The journey back didn't take as long as the search because now the group did not even pause to investigate anything. They hurried right on behind Uncle Ned and Uncle Wirt.

Once they reached Uncle Ned's house, everyone sat down in the kitchen, waiting to eat. The girls helped Morning Star serve the food, and soon everyone was eating heartily.

"Cat," Morning Star said to Mandie from the end of the table.

"Yes, I'll get Snowball down for his supper in a few minutes," Mandie replied, eating the beef stew in her plate.

As soon as everyone finished and sat back with a cup of coffee, Mandie decided it was time to go upstairs and get Snowball.

"I'll be right back," Mandie told her friends as she rose from the table. "I'm going to get Snowball."

She hurried upstairs to Sallie's room and opened the door, which was still tightly shut. "Snowball, where are you? Come on. Let's eat," she called to the cat as she looked around the room.

"Snowball, where are you?" Mandie asked, becoming anxious now since there was no sign of the white cat.

Quickly looking under the beds and in every nook and cranny in the room, she felt a sinking sensation. Snowball was missing. He was not in Sallie's room. How did he get out? The door had been closed.

Mandie hurried over to the room Joe was using and searched it, but no cat was found.

She felt like crying, but then, crying would not help. She took deep breaths and hurried back downstairs to report the missing cat.

Chapter 7 / Escapade in the Dark

Mandie hurried back into the kitchen, shouting loudly, "Snowball is gone! He's not in Sallie's room!" She stopped to stand by the table, where everyone was still sitting.

"Are you sure?" Joe asked, getting up from his chair.

"Didn't you close the door to my room when you put him in there?" Sallie asked.

"Oh, Mandie!" Celia exclaimed.

Uncle Ned cleared his throat and said loudly, "We find white cat." He spoke rapidly in the Cherokee language to Morning Star, who was puzzled by the excitement.

Morning Star quickly got up to come and put an arm around Mandie. "Cat be back," she said.

Mandie was embarrassed to find tears coming into her blue eyes, and she quickly turned to hug the old woman.

"I will help you look for him," Dimar said.

Riley O'Neal stood up and said, "Let's look for that white cat now before it gets dark."

Everyone agreed. Uncle Ned and Morning Star began searching the inside of the house. The others went outside.

"Don't forget to look up in all the trees. Snowball likes to climb trees," Mandie told them.

"Did he eat the food we put in the room?" Sallie asked.

Mandie thought for a moment and said, "I don't remember for sure, but I don't believe he ate any of it. As far as I remember, it was still there in the bowl."

"Then that means that cat got out a long time ago," Joe said. "That cat likes to eat, and all of the food would have been gone if he had stayed in the room very long."

Mandie thought about that and agreed, "Yes, he must have been out for a long time."

Riley O'Neal had taken over the search outdoors. "All right, now, let's go. You young ladies begin searching around the house and yard. The rest of us will fan out into the fields and woods."

Uncle Wirt, Joe, and Dimar followed him down the trail to the fields.

Mandie led the way, running as she searched behind every bush and looked up into every tree. She called loudly, "Snowball! Snowball, where are you? Snowball!"

They finally covered the yard and hurried out to follow Riley and his group. Joe and Riley had sticks with which they hit the bushes and the undergrowth. They finally all ended up by the creek on the other side of the cornfield and stopped to discuss possibilities.

"It is getting dark and we didn't bring any lanterns, so we must return to the house now," Riley O'Neal told them.

"Couldn't we go back and get lanterns and keep on going from here?" Mandie anxiously asked.

"Let's make that decision when we get back to the house," Riley replied.

"Maybe Uncle Ned and Morning Star have found him by now," Joe suggested as they started back toward the house.

"I don't understand how he got out of Sallie's room. I am positive we closed the door. It was still closed, so someone had to have let him out," Mandie said as she walked by Joe, Sallie, Celia, and Dimar.

"That cat has been missing before, and I don't believe we ever found him. He always came back on his own," Joe reminded her. "And if someone did let him out, they are long gone now."

"But who let him out? We were all gone," Mandie reminded him.

"Maybe someone we know came to see us and found no one home and went upstairs looking for us," Sallie suggested.

Mandie thought about that idea for a minute and then said, "No one ever locks their door around here, do they?"

"No one has ever had a key that I know of," Dimar said.

When they arrived back at the house, Uncle Ned and Morning Star had not found anyone around or a clue as to how Snowball got out.

"Must go home," Uncle Wirt said. "Back tomorrow."

"I must go home, also. My mother will be worried if I am late," Dimar said.

"We search tomorrow," Uncle Ned told Mandie. "Maybe white cat come home tonight."

Mandie was so worried about her cat that she would have liked to go back outside by herself and search some more, but she knew Uncle Ned would never allow it.

"Oh, where could Snowball be?" Mandie said, sitting in a chair in the kitchen as Riley, Dimar, and Uncle Wirt all said good-night and left.

"I'm sorry, Mandie," Celia said, sitting next to her.

Joe and Sallie pulled chairs up and sat down. Morning Star had cleared the table, but now she brought out a large pecan pie and told them, "Eat."

The young people quickly turned around to the table as Morning Star went to get the coffeepot on the stove. Sallie got cups, plates, and forks from the cabinet and set them on the table.

"My grandmother believes food is a cure for all worries," Sallie told them, smiling as Morning Star began filling the cups with coffee.

"Food certainly helps," Joe agreed.

Sallie cut the pie, put slices on the plates, and passed them around.

Mandie took a bite of pie from her plate and washed it down with a sip of coffee and then decided she was not hungry. She fiddled with the pie while her friends hastily ate, until suddenly Morning Star said very loudly, "Eat," and looked directly at Mandie.

Uncle Ned, sitting at the far end of the long table, heard this and echoed, "Eat." He frowned at Mandie. "Sin to waste food."

"Yes, sir," Mandie quickly replied, picking up her fork and cramming the pie down with swallows of the strong black coffee.

Too many things were happening, she was thinking. The quilt disappeared, and now her cat had also disappeared. And of course Tsa'ni was also not to be found, but who cared about that? The Indian boy did not like white people and was probably causing all this trouble to get even with someone.

Someone had to have taken the quilt, but who? Someone who knew their way around in Uncle Ned's house and who knew Mandie had brought it with her. She had not told anyone about it, but maybe someone saw it when Joe brought the valise containing the quilt into Uncle Ned's house.

And whoever took the quilt might have been the person who let Snowball out. She was sure an unknown person had opened the door to Sallie's room and allowed her cat to come out. And that person might be lurking nearby somewhere, evading the search.

Mandie would have been better off not to come to Uncle Ned's house. She would still have her white cat and the quilt if she had not changed her plans. However, one thing was for sure, she could not leave Uncle Ned's house now to go home until she found Snowball. And that might take quite a while to do. And Grandmother Taft was sitting there waiting for them to return so they could all go on to New York. And Mandie's mother was in New York and expected to see her soon.

Suddenly Celia, sitting next to Mandie, was pulling at her sleeve, asking, "Mandie, do you want more coffee?"

Mandie looked up and saw Morning Star standing there with the coffeepot, waiting to refill cups.

Quickly pushing her cup forward, Mandie looked up at Morning Star and said, "Just a little," and held up her fingers to measure how much.

Joe, sitting next to her, leaned over to say, "As

soon as we find that cat, we need to be going back to your house."

"I haven't even been to visit Uncle Wirt and Aunt Saphronia yet," Mandie replied.

"We can do that tomorrow," Joe said.

Mandie glanced at Uncle Ned and saw that he was looking directly at her. She always felt he could almost read her thoughts, so she asked, "Uncle Ned, are you going to Red Clay, Tennessee, tomorrow?"

"No, not go," the old man told her. "Later I go."

"Do you mean you are not going to Red Clay at all?" Mandie asked.

"Some other day. I stay, take you all home to John Shaw's," he explained with a smile.

"Oh, thank you, Uncle Ned, but I didn't want to interfere with your plans," Mandie said.

Her friends listened to the conversation.

"Not you, but Tsa'ni," Uncle Ned explained. "Waste time looking for him, not get other things done."

"I'm sorry," Mandie said. "After I visit Aunt Saphronia, we can all go back home, provided Snowball returns by then."

Joe and Celia both quickly looked at her. She knew they were thinking that she had given up on the whereabouts of the Cherokee quilt. She had not, but she wanted to see the quilts that Aunt Saphronia had made. And just maybe she would find the quilt somewhere. And if she didn't, maybe she could talk Aunt Saphronia into telling her what the message on the quilt was.

"Sleep now," Uncle Ned told the young people as he rose from his chair.

The young people said good-night and went

upstairs. They stopped at the door to Sallie's room to talk.

"We can leave the door to my room open so Snowball can come in if he returns during the night," Sallie said.

Long after Sallie and Celia were asleep, Mandie lay awake, trying to figure out what she should do next about her cat and the quilt. She suddenly realized she could faintly hear Snowball meowing somewhere. But where was he? She didn't want to wake her friends, so she cautiously sat up in bed and slipped out from under the covers. She held her breath to listen better. Sure enough, that was definitely Snowball's meow, but where was he? She cautiously moved about the room in the darkness, trying to figure out where the meow was coming from. As she passed the window and looked out, there was no sign of the white cat, but she could hear him better now. He was bound to be somewhere on the roof.

Being careful not to waken her friends, Mandie crawled out the window onto the roof in the darkness. She could finally determine the direction the meow was coming from.

"Snowball," she said in a whisper as she moved forward. Then she heard a swishing sound and looked back to see the window sliding shut all by itself. Oh well, she would get the cat and come back and raise it up so they could get back into the house.

She finally spotted the white cat. He was sitting next to the chimney and would not come to her. Going slowly over the steep roof, she made her way to Snowball. At last she could reach and pick him up. He was frightened and had his claws out, clinging to the rough boards on the roof.

"Snowball," Mandie whispered to him as she pulled his feet loose.

Once she had Snowball in her arms, she cautiously crawled back to the window to go inside. She had to set the cat down and use both hands in an effort to raise the window, but the window would not budge. Now what was she going to do? She couldn't get back in the house.

"We'll just have to go back and sit by the chimney where it's warm until Sallie and Celia wake up and let us back in," she whispered to the cat as she crawled back to the huge chimney.

The chimney was warm because the fire downstairs was never allowed to go out. Mandie cuddled up with her white cat against the warm rocks. She finally fell asleep and didn't wake until the sky had lightened up. She was cold and crampy when she opened her eyes. Snowball was still sleeping in her arms. Stretching, she put him down for a moment and said, "Snowball, we've got to get back into the house."

Once more she carried the cat across the roof and tried again to raise the window of Sallie's room. Sallie and Celia were both up inside and happened to see her. They came rushing to open the window, but it was still stuck.

"I'll get Joe," Celia quickly told Mandie through the glass, hurrying out of the room.

In a few moments Joe appeared in Sallie's room and managed to get the window sash up. Mandie pushed Snowball inside and then almost fell into the room herself. Sallie quickly placed Mandie's cloak around her.

"Mandie, what were you doing on the roof?" Celia asked in alarm.

"Snowball was on the roof," Joe said with a big grin.

"Yes, I heard him meowing," Mandie said and explained what had transpired.

"You should have let me know so I could help," Sallie told her.

"You shouldn't have gone out there yourself in the first place. All you had to do was let me know and I could have rescued the cat for you," Joe scolded her. "You could have fallen off and been killed."

"Oh, Mandie, I am so glad you're safe and that you have found Snowball," Celia said.

Snowball had jumped upon the bed Mandie slept in and was busily washing his face.

"I didn't want to wake anyone up," Mandie protested. "At least I found Snowball. And besides, it was not the first time I've ever been on a roof." She suddenly was shivering from cold and the delayed reaction of fright. She pulled her cloak closer around her.

"I'll wait in my room until you girls get ready to go downstairs," Joe said, going over to the door. "Just don't be too long. I'm hungry." He grinned at Mandie and then added, "And please don't let that cat out of your sight, not for a single moment."

"I don't intend to," Mandie replied.

As soon as Mandie was dressed, she knocked on the wall between the two rooms. Joe came back to join them as they went downstairs. Mandie carried Snowball.

"We'll go to see Aunt Saphronia today and then maybe tomorrow we'll go home," Mandie told Joe as they opened the kitchen door.

"Good," Joe replied.

Mandie, ahead of the others, stopped to turn

back and whisper to her friends, "Please don't tell anyone I was out on the roof."

The others nodded in agreement, and she led the way into the room.

Mandie had her white cat back. Now, if she could only find the quilt. Suddenly she had another idea. Maybe whoever put Snowball on the roof had also put the quilt up there. She'd have to look and see.

Chapter 8 / More Quilts

When the young people came into the kitchen, they found Riley O'Neal, Dimar, and Uncle Wirt already there. Morning Star had breakfast cooked and was preparing to serve it.

"White cat," Uncle Ned exclaimed. "Where find?"

Mandie set Snowball down, and he ran to hop into the woodbox behind the stove.

"Yes, where was he?" Riley also asked.

"He was on the roof outside Sallie's room, but we don't know how he got out there. The window was closed," Mandie explained as Morning Star motioned for everyone to sit down at the table.

They all pulled out chairs and sat down. Morning Star put food in a plate and set it down for Snowball, who immediately jumped out of the box and began devouring it.

"How did cat get on roof?" Uncle Ned asked, looking around the table.

Everyone shrugged their shoulders, and no one answered until Mandie said, "That's what I'd like to know. It either happened while we were gone on the search or after we came back while we were having supper."

"That lets all of us out," Joe reminded everyone. "We were all together on the search, and we were all here eating supper."

Mandie looked around the table. No one seemed to want to discuss this problem. They all acted as though they were in cahoots together about this. Did someone in this group know what happened, and if so, why weren't they speaking up?

"Maybe window open when put cat in room," Uncle Ned said, looking at Sallie.

"No, my grandfather, the window was closed," Sallie told him. "I always am sure to see the window is closed when I leave the room. I do not wish to have birds flying into my room through the window."

Mandie remembered hearing horse's hooves in the yard below night before last and mentioning it to Sallie yesterday morning. And she also remembered glancing at the window when she left Snowball in the room yesterday, and it had been closed.

Morning Star had been listening to the conversation and evidently didn't understand what was being said. She spoke to Uncle Ned, and he answered in their Cherokee language.

Sallie told Mandie, "My grandmother says she will stay here today and watch the white cat. You must go see your aunt Saphronia."

Mandie turned to smile at Morning Star and said, "Thank you, Morning Star, but I will take Snowball with me today."

Sallie translated that for her grandmother, who replied, and Sallie told Mandie, "My grandmother says the white cat is trouble for you to carry."

"Sallie, please explain that I will not let Snowball out of my sight again until we go home."

Sallie once again spoke to her grandmother, and Morning Star turned to smile at Mandie without commenting this time.

Uncle Wirt, eating his food quickly, said, "We go," to Mandie.

"Yes, sir," Mandie said. She turned to Celia and Joe and said, "I guess we'd better hurry and finish."

"Mandie, do you want me to go with you to your aunt Saphronia's house? Wouldn't you rather visit her by yourself?" Celia asked, finishing her cup of coffee.

"Yes, Celia is right," Joe added. "We could stay here and wait for you."

"No, no," Mandie quickly replied. "I want y'all to come with me." And almost whispering to Joe next to her, she added, "We might solve that mystery," meaning the missing quilt.

"All right, then," Joe agreed.

"Will we be coming back here today? Or should I take things to spend the night at their house?" Celia asked.

Mandie looked at Uncle Wirt and asked, "Will you bring us back today?"

The old man nodded his head as he rose from the table.

Riley stood up and said, "Since we don't have to search for a white cat today, I'd better get back and do some work."

"I will also go home," Dimar told Mandie. "I will return here tomorrow."

"And I will stay here," Sallie added. "My grandmother needs help cooking."

Uncle Wirt had brought his wagon, and the young people all piled aboard. Mandie held firmly to her white cat. As soon as they were on their way,

Mandie remembered she had planned to look on the roof to see if the quilt was up there. Now it would have to wait until they returned to Uncle Ned's.

When they arrived at Uncle Wirt's house, Aunt Saphronia was waiting for them in the doorway. Mandie jumped down from the wagon, grasping her cat in one arm and embracing her aunt with the other.

"Welcome," Aunt Saphronia greeted her as they hugged in the doorway. The old lady's face, full of wrinkles, broke into a happy smile. Then, turning to Celia and Joe, Aunt Saphronia spoke to them, "Welcome."

As they stepped into the front room of the house, Mandie was excited to see quilting frames set up in the corner and piles of material in various patterns and colors stacked next to it on a long table. Aunt Saphronia must be making quilts, and Mandie would be able to see how it was done. And perhaps she could mention the quilt with the mysterious message that her grandmother had made, or maybe Aunt Saphronia would say something about it.

"Oh, Mrs. Pindar, are you making a quilt?" Celia asked. "I've never learned how to do that."

Aunt Saphronia smiled at Celia and said, "Yes, I make, you watch." She went over to the pile of material and picked up a square piece of calico.

"Aunt Saphronia, I should learn how to make a quilt. I believe most of my Cherokee kinpeople know how," Mandie said, following the old woman across the room. She still held Snowball tightly in her arms.

"Long work, much time," Aunt Saphronia replied, looking at Mandie as she threaded a needle. "Sit, watch." She indicated a bench nearby.

"Oh no, not a quilt-making lesson," Joe moaned under his breath to Mandie.

Mandie glanced at him as he sat down on a stool. "You know why," she whispered back.

"Measure cloth, make lots same size," Aunt Saphronia said, holding up several of the squares of calico. "Make other color, same size, easy way." She held up a few of another stack of squares which were solid blue.

Mandie and Celia watched her closely. Aunt Saphronia made fast, tiny stitches close together as she joined a calico square to a blue one. Snowball, in Mandie's lap, tried to jump at the thread to catch it.

"Shut door, put cat down," Aunt Saphronia told Mandie, glancing at Snowball.

"Yes, ma'am," Mandie said, hurrying across the room to close the outside door and then releasing Snowball, who immediately came to sit by Aunt Saphronia and to watch the thread. Mandie sat back down and tried to watch Snowball and Aunt Saphronia at the same time.

The old woman finished joining the squares and smoothed them out on her lap. "See," she said. And picking up another calico square, she began attaching it to the other side of the blue square.

"Oh, I see what she is doing," Joe remarked with a little laugh. "She is making a checkerboard with calico squares and blue squares alternating."

Aunt Saphronia looked at him, smiled, and said, "Yes, but not always." When she had four squares sewn together, she laid them on the table and explained, "Not straight. Make crossways." She indicated the corners of the squares would point upward and the blocks would run at angles across the quilt when finished.

"I believe I could do that," Celia remarked.

"Long work, stitch, stitch, stitch," Aunt Saphronia explained. "Then make bottom side, stuff inside."

"Do you make other patterns, Aunt Saphronia?" Mandie asked.

"Yes," the old woman replied, nodding her head. "More patterns." She rose and went over to a huge chest at the other end of the room and raised the lid.

Mandie quickly followed her and saw stacks of quilts inside. She bent closer to look as Aunt Saphronia started pulling the quilts out. None of them resembled the mystery quilt she had found in the attic.

"Who made all these quilts, Aunt Saphronia?" Mandie asked.

"Lots people," the old woman replied. She held up a quilt with red flowers all over it. "I make this when young." She reached for another one as she laid that aside. "My mother make," she continued as she held up another quilt. This one had lots of circles made into it.

The girls looked closely at the quilts. Celia was interested in the handiwork. Mandie was watching for a quilt that might look like the one she had found, with odd symbols scattered over it.

"Here is one I can make easy pattern for you to make," the old woman said, holding up another one. This one had large blocks with crosses in the middle of each one.

Mandie quickly looked at this one and said, "It looks like people's names on the blocks."

"Yes, make quilt and people friends sign

name," Aunt Saphronia explained. "Long ago I make this one. Now I make simple pattern for you to make. Do you wish?"

"Oh yes, Aunt Saphronia, I'd love to make a quilt and have all my friends and relatives sign their names on it like that. But it looks awfully hard to make," Mandie explained.

Aunt Saphronia explained, "This called Album Block like this. I make pattern for you. Not so simple as Nine Patch Block, but I help. You can do it." She hurried over to the table, where her supplies were.

"Do you think I could really make a quilt?" Mandie asked, really interested now.

"And, Mandie, could I help you?" Celia asked.

"Yes, that way we'd get finished quicker," Mandie said with a big grin. Turning to Joe, she asked, "Do you want to help, too?"

Joe shrugged his shoulders and grinned back. "If I can be the first to sign my name on it," he replied.

"Now, we cut two squares light, eight squares dark," Aunt Saphronia explained as she began making a sample block. "Then cut one rectangle light, four rectangles dark." She quickly cut the blue and white pieces, laid them on the table, and showed Mandie how to make the strips that would form the cross in the center of each quilt block.

"Oh, I do believe I could do that," Mandie said excitedly.

"I will help you get started," Aunt Saphronia offered.

"But I don't want to take your cloth. Aren't you going to use that blue and the white for something else?" Mandie said.

"No worry. More in attic," Aunt Saphronia

replied, smiling at her. "Now we begin."

Mandie and Celia became so interested in quilt making, with Joe watching, that time flew. And suddenly Uncle Wirt came into the house.

"Must go now," the old man told Mandie and her friends. "Morning Star say be back to eat."

"Oh, I suppose we do have to go, Aunt Saphronia," Mandie told the old woman.

"Come back tomorrow. We work more," Aunt Saphronia said.

Mandie hugged her aunt, and Aunt Saphronia reached to include Celia and Joe in the embrace. "All come back tomorrow early, work all day," she said.

"Yes, ma'am, we will," Mandie promised, going over to pick up Snowball, who was asleep in front of the fireplace. Then looking at her friends, she said, "I wish we had told Morning Star that we would stay here all day today."

"We will tomorrow," Celia said.

Joe cleared his throat loudly and said, "Maybe Dimar and I will find something to do tomorrow while y'all make a quilt." He grinned at Mandie.

As they all piled into Uncle Wirt's wagon, Mandie asked the old man, "Has anyone found Tsa'ni yet?"

Uncle Wirt shook his head as he drove the wagon into the road. "No," he said. "Jessan back soon. He find."

Mandie grinned at Joe and said, "Maybe Joe and Dimar could look for Tsa'ni tomorrow while Celia and I learn to make a quilt with Aunt Saphronia."

Before Joe could reply, Uncle Wirt said quickly, "No look no more. Jessan find."

When they arrived back at Uncle Ned's,

Morning Star already had the noon meal cooked and ready to serve.

"Eat," the old woman told them as they came into the house.

"I go home," Uncle Wirt told her. "Back tomorrow." As he left the room, he waved his hand at Uncle Ned, who was sitting near the fireplace.

Sallie was helping her grandmother with the food. "I am glad you are back," she told Mandie and her friends as she laid silverware on the table.

"Oh, Sallie, I'm learning how to make a quilt," Mandie excitedly told her. She set Snowball down, and he immediately jumped into the woodbox behind the stove.

"I am, too," Celia added.

Grinning at Joe, Mandie said, "And so is Joe."

"No more," Joe said.

"We told Aunt Saphronia we'd come back tomorrow, Sallie. Can you go with us?" Mandie asked.

"We see," Sallie replied.

Uncle Ned stood up and came to the table. "Sit, eat," he told them.

"Eat," Morning Star echoed as she placed the last dish on the table.

Everyone sat down at the table. Morning Star began passing the bowls of food. Mandie, sitting next to Joe, saw him quickly examine the meat on a platter.

"That's ham," Mandie whispered to him.

"Ham and what else?" Joe said, still holding the platter.

"Turnips. Can't you smell them?" Mandie replied.

Joe quickly put some of the ham and turnips on his plate and passed it to Mandie.

"This looks good," Mandie said, placing some of the ham and turnips on her plate and passing the dish on to Celia.

Sallie had been watching and listening. She spoke up, "My grandmother knows you do not like owl stew. We will not cook owl stew while you are with us."

Joe cleared his throat and said, "Thank you, Sallie, for telling me that. I suppose nobody likes everything, so it just happens I don't like owl stew." He took a bite of the ham and turnips and added, "Now, this is delicious."

Everyone had paused to listen to the conversation when Morning Star suddenly said, "Eat," with a big smile. Everyone began eating.

Mandie looked down the table to Uncle Ned at the end and said, "Uncle Ned, Aunt Saphronia is teaching Celia and me how to make a quilt."

Uncle Ned looked at her for a moment and then said, "Make happy, good quilt."

"Yes, sir, it's going to be one that everyone signs their name on," Mandie explained. "Aunt Saphronia showed us lots of old quilts, and I decided I wanted to make a quilt."

"Good," he said, and then turning to Morning Star, he spoke rapidly in Cherokee.

Mandie watched as Morning Star first frowned and shook her head and then turned and smiled at Mandie. She then spoke to Sallie as she glanced at Joe.

Sallie translated, "Mandie, my grandmother says every girl should learn how to make a quilt, also boys should help."

"Please tell your grandmother, Sallie, that this boy is going to find Dimar and do some boy things with him, like maybe hunting," Joe said with a big grin directed at Morning Star.

Sallie rapidly repeated the message in Cherokee to her grandmother. Morning Star grinned,
nodded her head, and said, "Hunt, eat."

"Yes, ma'am, we'll go hunting and bring back
something to eat," Joe told her.

"We hunt tomorrow," Uncle Ned said, nodding
his head in agreement.

While the meal dragged on, Mandie became
impatient to get upstairs and search the roof for the
missing quilt. Whoever had shut Snowball out on
the roof might have also put the quilt out there,
hoping Mandie would never find it.

However, she had to delay her plans again as
Sallie made plans for them.

"After we finish eating, would you all like to
walk over to the Cherokee schoolhouse?" Sallie
asked the three young people. "I need to ask Mr.
O'Neal for a book."

"Yes," Celia and Joe both agreed.

"Of course, Sallie," Mandie added when she
could think of no excuse to delay their visit in order
that she might search the roof before they went.

As soon as they returned, she was definitely
going to search the roof.

Chapter 9 / Danger in the Dark

When the meal was over and the young people were preparing to walk over to the Cherokee schoolhouse, which was a short distance past the Cherokee hospital, Uncle Ned told Joe, "Take cart. Take firewood to school."

"Yes, sir, I'd be glad to. Where is the firewood?" Joe replied as he and Mandie waited for Sallie and Celia to wash their hands after helping to clear the table. Mandie held her white cat in her arms.

"Barn, back," Uncle Ned replied, motioning toward the back of his house. "Come." He led the way out the door and into the backyard.

Sallie and Celia caught up with them, and Sallie explained, "All our people chop wood and give it to Mr. Riley for the school. They bring it here to put in one pile, and whoever has time takes it to him."

They had all followed Uncle Ned into the barn in his backyard. He and Joe began loading the cart with wood from a bin in the corner.

"All this wood should last awhile," Mandie remarked.

"Yes, weather warm now," Uncle Ned replied.

"He still has to have wood to burn in his cookstove," Sallie added.

They got the cart loaded, hitched up the horse, and left for the Cherokee schoolhouse.

"This will not take long, since we are using the cart," Sallie said as Joe drove through the rough trail. "Perhaps we will find something else to do when we return to my grandfather's house."

"Maybe Dimar will be at your house when we go back and I can ask him about going hunting tomorrow with Uncle Ned and me," Joe said, slowing the horse to go down a steep slope.

"Dimar may be hunting for Tsa'ni with Mr. Wirt today," Sallie said.

"No," Mandie said, clutching Snowball, who was trying to get free. "Uncle Wirt said he would not search anymore and that Jessan could find Tsa'ni when Jessan gets back from Asheville."

"I wonder if Jessan has returned from Asheville," Celia said.

"He should have returned by now, but he has not been to my grandfather's house today if he did," Sallie explained.

"But maybe he has been out looking for Tsa'ni," Joe suggested. "I sure hope someone finds that boy, because I don't want to have to spend my time doing it."

"Yes," all three girls agreed at once.

Suddenly the wheels of the cart started sliding, and Joe pulled tightly on the reins. "Hold on," he told the girls.

In the sudden slowing of the cart, Snowball managed to get free from his mistress and jumped back into the woodpile, where he began howling as he stuck his claws into a piece of wood.

"Snowball, I can't reach you. You'll just have to hold on," Mandie called to him as the cart jolted and finally came to a stop.

"Sorry," Joe said, blowing out his breath and rubbing his hands together.

"We put too much wood on here for the steep road," Sallie told him.

Mandie reached back and grasped Snowball and pulled him to her. "Snowball, you are going to stay with me whether you like it or not," she told the cat.

Joe jumped down to look at the rough trail they had come over. He suddenly bent down to inspect a wheel. "I do believe we have a loose wheel," he told the girls, who also stepped down. Mandie held on to Snowball.

They all stooped to look as Joe pushed and pulled on a front wheel. "The nuts are loose," he told the girls. He straightened up and looked in the bed of the cart. "And we don't have any tools, do we?"

"No, I do not remember seeing any tools when we loaded the wood," Sallie replied.

"Sallie, how far are we from the schoolhouse?" Mandie asked. "Maybe we could walk on and get tools from Mr. Riley to come back and fix the wheel."

"There is a short cut," Sallie said. "It is not far if we walk."

"Then let's go. Show us the way, Sallie," Joe said.

Sallie cut through the woods, and the others followed. Soon they came into a large clearing.

"Look, there's the schoolhouse," Mandie said, pointing ahead. The log building was just barely visible through a thicket of bushes.

"Yes, we are almost there," Sallie agreed.

When they came out into another opening, the log schoolhouse stood before them.

Mandie stopped to look. "Is that a barn back there? Did Mr. Riley build a barn?"

As they continued on, Sallie replied, "Yes, since you were here all the men decided Mr. Riley needed a barn for his horse and for the firewood. They built it in three days." She smiled at Mandie.

"Three days," Joe exclaimed. "That was a quick job. It's a large barn, too."

"And it looks nice, too," Celia added.

The four walked on over to the barn and looked around inside. "His horse is not here," Sallie remarked. "Mr. Riley is not home."

Turning to Sallie, Joe asked, "Do you happen to know where Mr. Riley keeps his tools?"

"Yes," Sallie said, going to the far corner inside. "But do not tell the school children. He does not want them to handle the tools." She bent to open a small hidden door by the hay in the last stall.

Joe stooped to examine the tools inside the small bin. "Looks like he has some of everything," he remarked. "Let's see, I believe I need a wrench and this hammer, and maybe a screwdriver."

"Take as many as you need, Joe, because we can help carry them back to the cart," Mandie said, squeezing Snowball in her arms to keep him from getting down.

"I believe these will be enough," Joe said, standing up and pushing the door closed on the bin with his foot.

Sallie quickly pushed the hay back in front of the door, concealing it from view.

"Is there anything else we need to get?" Celia asked, looking around the barn. She quickly pulled a rag from a nail on the wall and said, "Like maybe something to clean your hands on." She smiled at Joe.

As they left the barn, Sallie looked around the yard and said, "Perhaps Mr. Riley will be home when we bring the wood."

"I hope so, after you came all the way over here to borrow a book from him," Mandie said.

The four young people returned to the cart, and Joe repaired the wheel. The girls watched as he tightened nuts and bolts until he was satisfied the wheel was secure. Then, taking the piece of rag Celia had brought, he vigorously wiped his hands and added, "Thanks for remembering to bring this. Now we will go unload this wood."

When Joe drove the cart up to the schoolhouse barn, Mandie saw a flash of something cross the yard behind it. Grasping Snowball, she jumped down and said, "There was someone back there." She hurried around the barn.

"Yes," Joe agreed.

"I saw something, too," Sallie added.

"It looked like someone running," Celia said.

The four of them gathered to look around the yard behind the barn. There was no sign of anyone now.

"Maybe there wasn't anyone after all," Joe said, frowning.

"No, Joe, I'm sure I saw something run toward the woods," Mandie declared. "And I don't believe it was an animal."

"There are lots of deer in this section," Sallie said.

"Whatever it was, I saw something," Celia said.

"Well, right now let's get this wood stacked in the bin," Joe told the girls as they entered the barn. "I believe I can get the cart closer so we won't have to carry the wood so far." He went back outside to move the cart up to the doorway.

When the four young people had transferred the wood to the bin inside the barn, there was still no sign of Mr. Riley. They stood around talking for a few minutes, discussing what they thought they had seen flitting through the yard. No one agreed on what it might have been.

"I suppose we should go on back to your grandfather's house, Sallie," Joe decided.

"Yes. But we must return Mr. Riley's tools to their place first," Sallie told him.

"Oh yes, I'm glad you reminded me," Joe said, walking over to the cart.

The girls came to help get the tools and carry them back inside.

Joe smiled at them and said, "You know, I could carry a screwdriver, hammer, and wrench all the way back to the bin." He laughed.

"We wanted to be sure they were put back in the right place," Mandie teased, grinning at him.

"Well, thank you," Joe said, grinning back.

When they were ready to leave, Joe glanced around the yard and said, "I'm sorry you didn't get the book you came after, Sallie."

"I will get it later," Sallie said. "I have been helping teach the little children, but none of them are attending school right now, so I have time to get the book later."

When they arrived back at Uncle Ned's house and related their adventures to him, he was concerned about the cart.

"Someone tinker with wheel," he said with a big frown. "I drive cart yesterday. All right."

"Then someone must have come into your barn since then," Mandie said.

Upon their return, Morning Star had immediately poured hot coffee, sliced a chocolate cake, and motioned for them to sit at the long table.

Mandie was beginning to think she would never get an opportunity to go upstairs and search the roof. At this house every minute seemed to be used in some way. She looked around the table and thought that maybe after everyone finished she could have a chance.

Then she looked up to see Dimar coming in the door. He was carrying something wrapped in a white cloth, which he held out to Morning Star.

"My mother sent this," Dimar told Morning Star.

Morning Star removed the cloth, and Mandie saw it was a huge bowl of white candy.

"We thank," Morning Star told Dimar and then spoke rapidly in Cherokee.

Dimar nodded and smiled and told the young people, "Morning Star was going to make a cake for you, and now she does not have to," he said.

"Sit," Uncle Ned said to Dimar.

Dimar sat down, and everyone began telling him about the episode with Uncle Ned's cart.

Dimar frowned and then said, "Tsa'ni is back."

Everyone understood what he meant. Tsa'ni was usually the cause of all the pranks and troubles around Deep Creek.

"Where had he been?" Mandie asked.

"I do not know. My mother saw Tsa'ni walk by our house this morning. He did not stop," Dimar explained.

Riley O'Neal came in the door. He smiled as he looked around the room and sat down as Morning Star motioned for him to do so.

"We came to see you and you were not home," Mandie said.

"Yes, I saw the wood and knew someone had

brought it, for which I wish to thank you, Uncle Ned," Riley said, turning to the old man.

Uncle Ned smiled and said, "Welcome."

Then the young people had to relate their adventures to Riley O'Neal.

"Yes, and I imagine you all saw Tsa'ni in my yard, because he brought a quilt and left it on the back stoop with a note saying it was from Aunt Saphronia. Remember Uncle Wirt said she would give me one? Well, I suppose since Tsa'ni is their grandson, they sent it by him," Riley explained. "Anyhow, I was glad to get it."

Mandie told Riley about their quilt-making with Aunt Saphronia that morning. "And we are going back tomorrow," she added.

Joe frowned and quickly said, turning to Riley O'Neal, "Please help me get out of this quilt-making business. Wouldn't you like to go hunting?" Turning to include Dimar, he said, "Both of you, tomorrow?"

Riley grinned and said, "Fine, we'll do that."

Dimar agreed also. And Uncle Ned reminded Joe he would be going, too.

Mandie was thinking, *At least all the men will be out of the way tomorrow so maybe I'll get a chance to search the roof then.*

But as luck would have it, Mandie got her chance that night. Dimar and Riley stayed for supper. Everyone had finished supper and was sitting around the table playing checkers when Mandie realized that everyone was occupied and she could slip upstairs.

"I'll be right back. I need to get something from upstairs," Mandie mumbled as she stood up and hurried toward the door. She left Snowball asleep in the woodbox behind the stove.

No one paid much attention to her, because all interest was on the checker game.

When she got upstairs in Sallie's room, Mandie quickly looked around for something to prop up the window so she could crawl out on the roof. Picking up one of Sallie's old shoes, Mandie went over, raised the window, slipped outside onto the roof, and turned back to stick the shoe under the window when it slid down, which she knew it would do.

Satisfied with this, she cautiously made her way across the roof in the darkness, brightened in spots by the moonlight through the trees, to the chimney. She looked around and also felt around in the darkness, but she did not find anything there. Looking beyond, she cautiously crept across the roof, examining it as she went.

Suddenly her foot slipped and she slid, falling down on her stomach and grasping for something to hold on to. The toe of her shoe stuck on a nail in the roof, and she took a deep breath as she wondered how she would ever get back up the steep roof and into Sallie's window.

Remembering her special verse in time of all kinds of trouble, Mandie whispered, " 'What time I am afraid I will put my trust in Thee.' " She knew God would answer and take care of her.

She lay there, afraid to move, for a long time. Then she decided she would have to try to make her way back across the roof. Afraid to stand up again, she crawled on her hands and knees for what seemed like hours to get back to the window of Sallie's room.

"At last!" she whispered as she finally came to the window. Slowly rising in order to slip back through the window, she suddenly realized the window was completely closed. The shoe that had propped it open was gone.

"Oh no!" she exclaimed, trying to push the window up. It was stuck and would not budge. She sat down to rest and think. How was she ever going to get back into the house?

She glanced across the roof and suddenly realized there was a window to the room that Joe was using. If she could only get to that, maybe it would open.

Inch by inch, she moved on her hands and knees toward the other window. Finally she was there. Slowly and carefully rising on her knees, she reached up to try the window. It moved at the touch of her hand. It would raise up.

"Thank you, dear Lord, thank you," she whispered in the darkness as she managed to push the window up enough to crawl through and fall to the floor inside. She lay there a moment, too tired and worn out to move.

Suddenly the door to the hallway opened and someone appeared carrying a lamp.

"Mandie, what are you doing? Are you all right?" It was Joe who was anxiously stooping over her.

"Oh, Joe, I'm sorry," Mandie muttered as she sat up and felt tears in her blue eyes in spite of everything.

"Mandie, what is it?" Joe insisted as he reached for her hand and set the lamp on the floor.

"Oh, Joe, I was out on the roof—" she began and took deep breaths to steady her voice. "And the quilt is not out there."

"Mandie, why didn't you tell me what you were doing?" Joe asked. "I could have looked for you. You could have been hurt out there."

Mandie bent her head against her knees in order to hide her tears and said, "I'm sorry, Joe."

"We'll find that old quilt yet, but please don't take any more dangerous chances," Joe said, reaching to smooth Mandie's blond hair. "After all, you promised to marry me when we grow up, and at this rate we may not live to grow up." He laughed loudly.

Mandie joined the laughter and said, "I won't go out on that roof again. I promise. But I do need to find that quilt."

"I'll help you," Joe promised.

Mandie silently wiped the back of her hand across her face to clear the tears. Together they would find that quilt.

Chapter 10 / Another Quilt Mystery

The next morning everyone met in the kitchen for breakfast. Riley and Dimar came to join Uncle Ned and Joe in a hunting trip over the mountain. Uncle Wirt came to take Mandie and Celia to his house to continue their quilting lessons.

As they sat around the long table having breakfast, Mandie asked Sallie, "Won't you come with us to Aunt Saphronia's? We may be gone all day, and I'd like to spend some time with you since we will be leaving soon."

"I am not sure," Sallie said. Turning to her grandmother, she spoke in the Cherokee language for a few moments.

Then Morning Star spoke rapidly to Uncle Ned in their language.

The old man replied to her and then turned to Joe, Riley, and Dimar. "Morning Star say go fish. She go, too," Uncle Ned told them.

"Fish?" Joe asked and looked at the others.

"Yes, my mother could use some fish," Dimar agreed.

"Yes, we could go fishing," Riley said.

"It really doesn't matter to me what we do, as long as I don't have to go with the girls for that quilt-making lesson," Joe said, grinning at Mandie.

Uncle Ned turned to Uncle Wirt and asked, "You fish, too?"

Uncle Wirt grunted and said, "Yes."

"But you will take us to your house first, won't you, Uncle Wirt?" Mandie asked.

"Yes, first," the old man agreed, drinking a cup of coffee.

"And I will go with you," Sallie told Mandie. "Since my grandmother is going fishing, I will not be needed here today." She began eating hurriedly.

Mandie swallowed a bite of ham and asked, "Uncle Wirt, Tsa'ni did come home, didn't he? Do you know where he had been?"

"Tsa'ni say he followed Jessan to Asheville, but Jessan did not see him until he came home yesterday," Uncle Wirt explained.

"But he did come to your house, didn't he? He brought me a quilt yesterday and left it on the back stoop with a note saying it was from your wife," Riley told him.

"Yes, she give him quilt and say take to school," Uncle Wirt replied.

"I had gone across the mountain to take some books to some of the children over there who attend our school. I am really worried that the Cherokee children always seem to find excuses not to go to school," Riley said. "I've been thinking, if you would agree, that if you had a little meeting with some of the parents, you might be able to get the children back in school. What is your opinion? Would a meeting help?"

"Yes, we have powwow. Soon," Uncle Wirt agreed.

"And since Sallie is teaching some of the children, maybe she could come to the meeting, too.

That would show the parents that it is not a white school but is a special school just for Cherokee children," Riley said.

"Yes, Sallie come to powwow, too," Uncle Wirt agreed.

"Uncle Wirt, do you plan on having this meeting while I am here?" Mandie asked. "I'd like to go, too."

The old man smiled at her and shook his head. "Too soon. Need more time to make powwow," he replied. "Must talk and talk to get powwow."

Sallie said to Mandie, "It will take lots of talk to get the parents to come to such a meeting. They are not interested in whether their children go to school or not. Most of the parents did not go to school."

"Oh, I wish I could help," Mandie said with a sigh.

"Parents will only listen to Mr. Wirt because he is the eldest in our settlement," Sallie explained.

"Does Tsa'ni go to school?" Mandie asked.

"Sometimes," Riley O'Neal replied.

Uncle Wirt shook his head and frowned as he said, "Tsa'ni need school bad."

"I go to school when it is in session," Dimar said, glancing at Riley O'Neal. "But it is not in session very much."

"Yes, but you do study your books at home," Riley reminded him. "And you are making good progress."

"One must have the desire to learn, and I have that desire," Dimar told him.

"We must think of some way to give that desire to the children who do not wish to go to school," Sallie said.

"How about a hickory switch? That's what the white children would get if they didn't go to school," Joe said with a big grin.

"It is the parents we must convince," Sallie said. "The children will go to school if the parents require them to."

Uncle Wirt stood up from the table and said, "We go now," as he looked at the girls. Turning to Uncle Ned, he added, "Back soon."

"We wait," Uncle Ned replied.

Mandie hurried to pick up Snowball, who had finished his breakfast and was washing his face by the stove. As she started to follow the other girls out the door, Joe caught up with her and whispered, "You won't go off somewhere looking for that quilt, will you?"

"I won't," Mandie promised, and then added, "Not on any more roofs, anyhow." She smiled at him.

"Not just roofs," Joe said. "No place except to your Aunt Saphronia's and back here."

"We're going to Aunt Saphronia's to learn how to make a quilt, so we won't have a chance to do anything else," Mandie reminded him.

"I don't know whether we will return before you do or not," Joe said.

"Since Uncle Wirt is going with y'all, he'll have to come back to get us to bring us home. So I imagine you'll be back before we are," Mandie told him. She held tightly to her white cat.

"Anyhow, please stay out of trouble," Joe said.

"Come on, Mandie," Celia called from the open doorway.

Sallie and Uncle Wirt had already gone outside. "I'm coming," Mandie replied and hurried to join her friend, smiling back at Joe as she went.

On their way to join Sallie and Uncle Wirt at the wagon, Mandie whispered to Celia, "Joe is afraid

I'll go off somewhere and get in trouble looking for that quilt." She had told Celia about the escapade on the roof the night before.

"He knows you do get in trouble lots of times chasing down mysteries," Celia reminded her as they got to the wagon and climbed aboard.

Since Mandie had not told Sallie about the missing quilt, she could not say anything more. She held on to Snowball as Uncle Wirt drove the wagon at a fast speed to his house.

Aunt Saphronia was waiting for them at the back door, and Mandie caught a glimpse of a large chocolate cake with dishes stacked nearby on the table as they went through the kitchen into the front room, where the old woman did her sewing.

"Close door. Put cat down," Aunt Saphronia told her.

Mandie quickly went back to close the outside door to the kitchen. Then she put down Snowball, who immediately headed for the woodbox behind the huge cookstove. She left the door to the kitchen open as she followed Aunt Saphronia, Celia, and Sallie.

"Now we work," Aunt Saphronia said, sitting down at her worktable. She reached for a stack of blue material cut into squares.

"Aunt Saphronia, Uncle Wirt said Tsa'ni came home yesterday and you sent a quilt by him to the schoolhouse for Mr. Riley," Mandie said as she and her friends drew up stools to sit down.

"Did Tsa'ni not take quilt to school?" the old woman asked, turning to look at Mandie.

"Yes, ma'am, he took it. Mr. Riley was at Uncle Ned's this morning and said he did," Mandie replied.

"Good. Now we work," the old woman told her.

Mandie was good at making the tiny stitches

required on the blocks, but she was terribly slow because her mind kept wandering off to the missing quilt. Where would she look next for the quilt? They couldn't stay much longer at Uncle Ned's, because her grandmother expected them back home to go with her to New York. Joe had said he would help Mandie look for the quilt. But then, Joe never had any ideas about how to solve any mystery, so she would have to come up with plans.

"Coffee," Aunt Saphronia told the girls, rising from her chair.

Mandie came back to the present and realized they were taking a break to go into the kitchen for cake and coffee. She smiled to herself as she followed the others. *Joe sure missed out on this chocolate cake.*

The girls helped Aunt Saphronia fill the coffee cups and bring them to the table, where the old lady began slicing the cake, placing it on plates, and passing it around.

"Sit. We talk," Aunt Saphronia told them.

After they were all seated, Aunt Saphronia continued, "You learn how to make quilt?" She looked at the three girls.

"Yes, ma'am, so far," Celia replied.

"Yes, my grandmother has already taught me some patterns," Sallie said.

Mandie thought about it for a moment and then said, "I can make the blocks, but I'm not sure I can put it all together to make a quilt."

"That take days to do whole job," Aunt Saphronia said. "I show you how make blocks. Learn more when you go home."

"But I don't know anyone at home who can make quilts," Mandie replied, frowning as she thought about various people.

Then Aunt Saphronia surprised her. "John Shaw, son of Talitha, know how," she said with a big smile.

Mandie gasped in surprise. "Do you mean my uncle John knows how to make quilts? Him?" she asked.

Aunt Saphronia, still smiling, replied, "Yes, Talitha teach him."

Mandie immediately thought of the lost quilt. She was sure her uncle had seen the quilt when she and her friends had found it in the attic. He had not made any comment on the pattern, but she wondered if he had been able to read the message on it. After all, he was one-half Cherokee and knew the language.

"Do you know if he actually made any quilts?" Mandie asked. She was so eager to ask Aunt Saphronia about the missing quilt but was afraid to. After all, it had been her husband who had sent it back and said to put it away.

"Not know. That many years ago. You ask him," Aunt Saphronia said. Sipping her coffee, she continued, "I give all you white cloth. You take home and sew. Then get names signed."

"You mean we should make the quilt blocks before we get people to sign?" Celia asked.

Aunt Saphronia smiled at her, nodded her head, and said, "Yes, not time to make here. We make few but not enough."

They went back to work until they stopped for the noon meal of stew and cornbread, which Aunt Saphronia had already cooked. Then they once again continued making quilt blocks until Uncle Wirt came home with the fish he had caught.

Handing the bucket of fish to Aunt Saphronia, he told the girls, "Morning Star say bring you back."

Aunt Saphronia quickly set the fish in the dry

sink and told the girls, "Must get blocks take with you."

"Oh, but I want you and Uncle Wirt to sign two of my quilt blocks for me," Mandie told her as she followed Aunt Saphronia into the front room to get their things. Celia and Sallie and Uncle Wirt came in behind them, with Snowball meowing wildly at the smell of fish in the kitchen.

"We sign," Aunt Saphronia replied, going over to get the white material. Turning back to Wirt, she said, "We sign quilt."

Uncle Wirt took down a bottle of ink and a pen from the top shelf over the fireplace. He brought it over to the worktable.

While the girls watched, the two old people slowly wrote their names on blocks for each of the three.

"Thank you," Mandie said, surveying the work and then turning to hug Aunt Saphronia.

"And I thank you," Celia said with a big smile.

"I thank you," Sallie added, picking up her pieces of material. "Do not touch the name till it's dry," she warned the other two girls.

Uncle Wirt took the girls back to Uncle Ned's house. Mandie had to hold on to Snowball with one hand because she held her quilt blocks and material in the other. Snowball had not wanted to come with them. He had wanted to stay where the fish were.

Uncle Wirt let them out at Uncle Ned's and went back home.

Morning Star already had the fish cleaned and ready to fry when they arrived. The three girls immediately took advantage of everyone being together and demanded everyone sign a quilt block. Everyone but Joe and Riley O'Neal understood what they were doing.

"You just sign your name on a quilt block, and I will sew it into a quilt when we get home," Mandie explained. "This is called the Album Block, and you are supposed to get all your friends to sign on the white crosses."

Sallie got the pen and ink, and everyone had to sign a block for each girl's future quilt. Mandie was surprised to learn that Morning Star did know how to sign her name, even though she spoke very little English.

"I taught my grandmother," Sallie said as Mandie watched Morning Star sign her name.

"She does a good job," Mandie said.

Morning Star shooed everyone except Sallie out of the kitchen so she could prepare supper. Mandie, Joe, and Celia went to sit on the back steps. Snowball stayed around Morning Star's feet, hoping for a piece of fish.

Mandie told Joe they had learned that her uncle John Shaw knew how to make quilts.

"And I've been wondering if he knew what the message was on the quilt we found. I'm sure he saw it, but I don't know whether he noticed that it had a message on it, like Uncle Ned said," Mandie told Joe.

"I don't know, but I would never have thought Mr. Shaw knew how to quilt," Joe said with a big grin.

"I suppose we are going to have to go home in a day or two. Grandmother is waiting for us," Mandie said. "And if we don't find the quilt before we leave here, that will worry me forever."

Joe grinned at Mandie and said, "But Mandie Shaw is always able to solve any mystery she runs into."

"Yes, you are right about that," Celia agreed.

"But this time I just don't know what to do next,"

Mandie said, frowning as she thought about it.

And she thought about it all during supper and afterward as everyone played checkers again. Dimar had taken his fish home to his mother, but Riley had stayed to join Uncle Ned's family.

Finally Riley O'Neal went home, and everyone went to bed. The three girls went upstairs to Sallie's room together. As soon as she stepped into the room, Mandie spotted her valise back in the corner where she had originally left it. Without a word she rushed over to it, peeped inside, and found a quilt that she had never seen before. Someone had switched the quilts.

Trying to catch Celia's attention without Sallie seeing, Mandie said, "I need something out of my valise." And she went over to the returned valise. While Sallie was not looking, Mandie made faces and pointed to the valise.

Celia cleared her throat as she watched and said, "Yes, I need to get my hairbrush." She reached into her own valise for the brush as she nodded to Mandie.

Snowball had come upstairs with them. Suddenly he began meowing and clawing at the valise. Mandie hurried over to pick him up. "You be quiet now, Snowball. It's time to go to bed," she scolded the cat as she set him on the bed.

The cat jumped down from the bed and went racing back over to the valise.

Sallie noticed and said, "Do you think he believes that is his sandbox?"

"I don't know," Mandie said, picking him up again. This time she set him down in his sandbox in another corner. He scratched and used the box. Then Mandie picked him up and got in bed and held on to him. He finally hushed.

Later, when Mandie thought Sallie was asleep, she whispered to Celia, "It has the wrong quilt in it."

"It is your valise, though, isn't it?" Celia whispered back sleepily.

"Yes," Mandie replied.

Celia drifted off to sleep, and Mandie lay awake trying to figure out how the valise got back into the room and why it had the wrong quilt in it.

She could hardly wait to tell Joe about this, but she knew she didn't dare get up and go to his room in the night.

Then something else finally dawned on her. The quilt must smell like fish, since Snowball had gone wild over it. That meant someone with fish had put it there. And she knew who all had gone fishing that day—Dimar, Riley, Uncle Ned, Morning Star, and Uncle Wirt. Could it have possibly been one of them? She instantly felt that Uncle Wirt was the one involved in this. After all, he had been the one who demanded that she put the quilt away.

But then, how would Uncle Wirt have known she had the quilt with her?

"Oh, but these Indians are smart. They know everything that goes on," she mumbled under her breath.

Now the problem was to find the quilt with the message. If Uncle Wirt had taken it, she might never find it, because he didn't want her to know what the quilt said.

Mandie fell asleep and dreamed the quilt was back in the valise.

Chapter 11 / Discoveries

The next morning Mandie woke early and quietly dressed. She hurried down to the kitchen, hoping to find Joe also up so she could talk to him. She took Snowball with her, remembering his interest in her valise. Downstairs, the white cat ran for the woodbox as usual and hopped in.

Joe was already in the kitchen. He and Uncle Ned were drinking coffee.

"Sit," the old man told her. "I get coffee for you." He stood up.

"No, sir, not right now, Uncle Ned. I'd like to go outside and get a breath of fresh air first, and then I'll have coffee with you," Mandie replied with a big smile.

"I was about to refill my cup, but I believe I'll go with you for a walk in the yard," Joe told her as he rose.

"Uncle Ned, do you want to go outside with us?" Mandie asked, guessing that he would not be interested.

The old man shook his head and sat back down. "Not now," he said.

Once outside, Mandie quickly told Joe about the strange quilt in her valise. "And it smells like fish," she said. "Snowball had a fit trying to get the valise open."

"Everyone went fishing yesterday except you girls, so that would be hard to trace," Joe reminded her. "But if that's not your quilt in the valise, I wonder where the other quilt came from, who owns it."

"Yes, that's what I'm trying to figure out," Mandie said.

"What are you going to do with this quilt? I mean, you aren't going to take it home in your valise, are you?" Joe asked.

"Oh no, never," Mandie quickly replied. "I had not thought about that, but I will have to take it out of my valise so I can take my valise home when I go."

"Maybe you could just hide it in a corner of the barn or somewhere," Joe suggested. "When someone finds it, we will be gone and no one will know you put it there."

"Yes, I could do that," Mandie agreed. "But I'm hoping I can find the other quilt before we have to leave."

"Tomorrow is Sunday," Joe reminded her. "Don't you think we ought to go home to your house tomorrow? That way we could be ready to go to New York on Monday and still have a few days up there with your mother and the others."

"And maybe your parents have gone to New York since we didn't go when we said we were going," Mandie reminded him. "And since they had planned to come out here with us."

"I suppose we should go back inside now," Joe said.

"Yes," Mandie agreed as they started walking back toward the door. "Will you keep an ear out for anything that might be connected with this new quilt?"

"Of course," Joe agreed.

When they went back inside, Uncle Ned was still in the kitchen. And Morning Star was there, beginning breakfast. Sallie and Celia came in the other door.

"Outside so early?" Celia asked.

"Yes, it's going to be a beautiful spring day," Joe replied.

"Sit," Morning Star said, waving them to the table. "Coffee."

"Yes, ma'am," Mandie said. "I could drink some coffee now."

Sallie helped her grandmother prepare breakfast while everyone else sat and drank coffee.

"Celia, Joe thinks we ought to go home tomorrow and then on to New York on Monday. What do you think?" Mandie asked.

"Whatever y'all want to do is fine with me. However, my mother did have me promise to be sure to get to New York so we could do some shopping," Celia replied, pushing back her long curly auburn hair.

"They are supposed to stay in New York through next week, I believe," Joe said.

Celia nodded in agreement. "Yes," she said.

Riley O'Neal came in through the back door. Taking off his wide-brimmed hat, he greeted everyone. "Good morning, good morning," he said, and as Morning Star looked at him, he added, "I didn't come for another free breakfast. I've already had mine." He returned her smile.

Morning Star, who understood very little English, motioned to him and to the table as she said, "Sit."

"Uncle Ned, will you help me out? I know Morning Star didn't understand what I said, but it would be impossible for me to eat another breakfast," Riley told the old man.

Uncle Ned smiled at him and spoke to Morning Star in Cherokee.

Morning Star waved her hand toward the table again and said, "Sit."

Riley grinned at her and said, "Yes, ma'am," as he pulled out a chair and sat down next to Uncle Ned. Morning Star spoke to Sallie, and Sallie hurried over with a cup of coffee and set it in front of him. "Thank you," he told her.

"You'd better drink that coffee, or Morning Star is liable to get awfully put out with you," Joe teased.

"I'll drink the coffee, all right. She makes delicious coffee," Riley replied. Turning to Mandie, he said, "I came to ask a favor of you."

"Me?" Mandie asked. Then smiling, she said, "What can I do for you?"

"You said you'd like to help in getting the Cherokee children back to school," Riley began. "I'm planning to distribute dozens and dozens of school papers among the Cherokee people. I'm making up a simple lesson in arithmetic and in English grammar and would like to pass a copy out to anyone who will accept it. Even though the children may not want to do the lesson, I believe they will be curious enough to read it. And of course they will all have to be handwritten, since we don't have a printing press."

"Oh yes, I'll help. That sounds like a good idea," Mandie replied.

"I will also help," Celia volunteered.

"And so will I," Joe added.

Riley looked at the three, smiled, and said, "I never hoped for such good luck. As you all know, this will take a lot of time, so when can you begin?"

"Now," Mandie replied. "As soon as we eat breakfast. I don't believe Morning Star would let us get away from her without eating." She laughed.

"I'll wait then, and you all can go back with me," Riley told them.

Sallie had overheard the conversation as she tended pots on the stove and asked, "Do you need me to help, also?"

"No, Sallie. I've brought those books you've been wanting to study in preparation for teaching the next class we can get together. They're in my cart. I'll get them," Riley said, hurrying out the back door.

"Sallie, are you still going to school yourself, or just teaching the little children?" Mandie asked.

"Yes, I still go to school. I am in class with Dimar. However, the school is really out for the summer vacation right now, and we had hoped we could persuade the little ones to come and learn during the summer," Sallie explained.

Riley O'Neal came back into the kitchen with two books, which he handed to Sallie, saying, "Here are the books. I have already taken lessons out of them for the papers I plan to give out. I'll give you a copy when we get finished."

"Thank you," Sallie said, taking the books and flipping through the pages as she sat down at the end of the table.

"Eat," Morning Star announced as she brought dishes of food to the table.

The young people, anxious to get on with the work for Riley, hurried through the meal. As they started to leave, Morning Star came to the door with them and said, "Back, eat," and turned to speak to Sallie in Cherokee.

Sallie smiled and said, "My grandmother says you should all return here for the noon meal because school man does not know how to cook for you."

Everyone howled with laughter as Riley O'Neal's face turned red.

"Ask your grandmother why I should learn to cook when I can always get such wonderful meals here." Riley replied, smiling at Morning Star.

Sallie translated for her grandmother, who immediately began talking in Cherokee. Everyone stood still, waiting.

"My grandmother says you teach the children, and someone should teach you how to cook," Sallie said. "Someday you may have a wife."

"Let's go!" Riley exclaimed, rushing out the door, laughter following him.

Mandie knew Riley was not much older than Joe. However, he had had a formal education up north in Boston and seemed much older. Now she gave Joe credit over Riley. At least Joe knew how to cook. She knew from visits to his house.

As soon as they arrived at the schoolhouse, Riley gave each one of them a paper to copy and the three set to work.

"These should be printed in block letters because a lot of the children cannot read handwriting," he explained as they sat together on a long bench at one of the homemade tables. He placed a stack of blank paper before them. He sat down at one end, saying, "I will also be making up some of these."

"This shouldn't take a long time," Mandie said, looking over the sample pages.

"Long enough that you may want some coffee, which I do know how to make, and some cookies that Morning Star gave me when she baked a few days ago," Riley replied. "I also have a spring-house down by the creek where I keep milk and other things."

"It sounds like you are self-sufficient," Joe remarked.

"We will return to Morning Star's for the noon-day meal, however," Riley said, and then added, "She is a better cook than I am."

"She is the best cook I know of except for Aunt Lou at our house," Mandie said. Then, looking at the paper she was copying, she asked, "Will you be asking for the name of anyone who fills out one of these? Should we make a place to put their name?"

"No, I'd already thought about that and felt more people would fill these out if they didn't have to put their name on it," Riley explained. "I just hope we do get a few back."

"I believe you will," Celia said.

They worked as rapidly as they could making the block letters. After a couple of hours Riley put the percolator on the stove in his living quarters, which was a large room attached to the school-house. He set out the cookies, and everyone paused for a break.

Mandie flexed her fingers and said, "It would be nice if I could write with both hands. Making block letters is so much slower than handwriting."

"At the rate we're going, we should be finished sometime after the noonday meal," Riley said. "Morning Star expects us back at twelve o'clock, and we should be back here by one-thirty or two o'clock. Then I'd say another hour or two should complete the job."

When they stopped again, this time to go to Uncle Ned's house to eat, Joe asked the girls, "Have y'all decided whether you want to go home to Mandie's house tomorrow so we can leave for New York on Monday?"

They all climbed into Riley's cart.

"Yes, I suppose we have to," Mandie said regretfully.

"That's fine with me," Celia agreed.

"We need to let Uncle Ned know so he can prepare to take us," Joe said.

"All right, go ahead and tell him, then, Joe," Mandie said.

As he shook the reins and started the cart down the road, Riley said, "Sure sounds like an interesting journey, going all the way to New York. I've only been back to Boston once since I came here."

Mandie explained about their friends the Guyers in New York, where they would be staying. "It's nice to visit up there, but everything is too big and noisy to live there," she said.

"I agree with that. This part of the country here is so nice and peaceful and full of wide-open spaces," Riley said. "I don't think I'd ever want to go back to Boston to live, even though my family is there."

"You have a family?" Joe asked.

"Of course," Riley said, laughing. "I have a mother and a father and two sisters who all live in Boston, besides countless cousins and aunts and uncles and such."

"You're an only son, then. Didn't your father want you to stay near him?" Celia asked.

Riley laughed again and said, "No. He is a

minister and had hoped I would follow in his footsteps, but when I decided to become a missionary, he was enthusiastic about it."

"I never think of you as a missionary, but as a schoolteacher," Mandie said.

"But I am both," Riley said. "I work for the missionary board back in Boston, and they have different fields of work going on in a lot of places."

"My father is a doctor, but I am studying toward a law degree," Joe said.

"And what about you young ladies?" Riley asked, glancing at Mandie and Celia as he drove the cart.

"I may go into music," Celia replied.

"Music? When did you decide that?" Mandie asked in surprise.

"I didn't decide. I'm only thinking about it," Celia replied. "Since we've been taking music at our school, I've become interested. Maybe opera."

Mandie really did gasp at that. She finally found her voice to say, "Opera? Oh, Celia, that would be a great career, but what about Robert?" Then she realized she shouldn't have said that before other people.

Celia's face turned red as she said, "Oh, Robert, he's just a schoolmate."

"Well, anyhow, right now I don't know what I want to do," Mandie said, feeling awful for mentioning Robert.

Joe looked at Mandie and frowned. She wouldn't meet his eyes.

Morning Star had the food ready, and they sat down for the noon meal.

"Uncle Ned," Joe began from down the table. "If it is convenient with you, I suppose we'd better be going back to Mandie's house tomorrow so we can go on to New York with her grandmother."

Uncle Ned nodded and said, "Leave sunup."

The old man had been a dear friend of Mandie's father. Although he was not really blood related, he had promised Jim Shaw when he died that he would look after Mandie. And Mandie was thinking now how much she loved him. He always seemed to drop everything else to look after her.

"Thank you, Uncle Ned, for bringing us out here to your house and for taking us back to my house," Mandie told him with a big smile.

Uncle Ned only smiled back at her.

As soon as the noon meal was finished, Mandie, Joe, and Celia went back to the schoolhouse with Riley to finish their job of printing lessons for the Cherokee children.

True to Riley's estimate, they finished a couple of hours later. They carefully inspected what they had done and gave the papers to Riley.

"Let's have a cup of coffee before we return to Uncle Ned's," Riley suggested, rising from the table. "I'll put these in my room, where no one will be able to get them ahead of time." He took the papers and started toward the door to his room.

Mandie happened to glance at him and saw one of the papers flutter to the floor as he went. She jumped up, retrieved it, and followed him to the doorway. "Here, you dropped one," she said, glancing beyond him into the room. Suddenly she exclaimed loudly, "Oh no!"

Joe and Celia came hurrying to see what was wrong. Riley had gone on into the room, but Mandie had paused at the doorway.

"Look!" Mandie cried, so excited she could barely speak. "The quilt!"

Her friends looked, and there on Riley's chair was the missing quilt.

Riley turned back to look at them. "What is it? What's wrong?" he asked.

"You have my quilt!" Mandie exclaimed, walking into the room and to the chair. She ran her hand over the half-folded quilt.

"Your quilt?" Riley asked. "That's the quilt Tsa'ni left on my back doorstep. Does it belong to you?"

Mandie could tell Riley was completely confused about the quilt. She tried to explain how they had found it in her attic at home and Uncle Ned had taken it off to Uncle Wirt to read the message.

"And Uncle Ned brought it back to me and wouldn't tell me what the message is on the quilt," Mandie said, out of breath with excitement. "That's why we came to visit here. I thought maybe I could get one of my Cherokee kinpeople to translate the message on the quilt for me."

"The quilt has a message?" Riley asked, quickly shaking out the folds of the quilt. Then he also became excited. "It certainly does."

"Do you know anyone who would tell us what it says?" Mandie asked.

Riley looked at her and said, "You don't need anyone to do that. Remember, I have been here long enough to have learned to read the Cherokee language myself—but not to speak it." He turned back to the quilt.

"What does it say, Riley?" Joe asked.

"Do tell us," Celia added.

Mandie held her breath, waiting for Riley to speak. When he turned back to her, he asked, "Who made this quilt? Where did it come from?"

"My grandmother, Talitha Pindar Shaw, made

it. She died in 1863. If you can read it, what does it say?" Mandie asked impatiently.

Riley cleared his throat and said, "I hate to tell you. However, you do have a right to know, if she was your grandmother. She was full-blooded Cherokee, and your grandfather was a white man, right?"

"Yes, what does it say?" Mandie asked again.

"There is the date on here, 1838, which was during the Cherokee removal," Riley said.

"Yes, that's when she met my grandfather. They were married later," Mandie explained. "The quilt was made before she met him. I know that much about it."

"All right, then, here's the message," Riley finally agreed to tell her. He bent closer to examine the quilt.

Mandie stared at the quilt, which had a black background with various symbols and birds scattered over it. How could anything like that be translated into English?

"It is a message to the effect that all white people should be killed in this land of the Cherokee people because white people are stealing their land," Riley said. "It has many hate symbols on it." He straightened up to look at Mandie.

Mandie felt pains go through her heart. Her grandmother had hated white people. She was Mandie's father's mother, and she hated white people. Mandie suddenly felt like throwing up.

Riley reached for the percolator on the stove, poured a cup of coffee, and held it out to Mandie. "Sit down. Drink this," he said.

Mandie sank into the nearest chair and took the cup. With shaking hands, she managed to sip the coffee.

No one said a word for a few minutes. Then Joe spoke, "Mandie, remember, this quilt was made before your grandmother met your grandfather."

"But she hated white people. How could she marry a white man?" Mandie argued.

"I understand now what all the secrecy about the quilt was," Celia said. "No one wanted you to know the message for fear it would hurt you."

"You say you found this quilt in your attic at home," Riley said. "Do you live in the same house where your grandmother lived when she was married to your grandfather?"

"Yes," Mandie said, trying to control her sobs.

Joe explained, "Mandie's great-grandfather built the house, and he had lots of Cherokee friends. When the removal started, he built a special tunnel in his house to hide his Cherokee friends from the white soldiers who were forcing them to move out of the country there."

"And it was then that Mandie's grandmother and grandfather met," Celia added.

"And she probably married my grandfather to keep the white soldiers from forcing her to leave the country there," Mandie said. "And all the time she hated him and all his white kinpeople."

"Isn't Uncle Wirt her brother? I'm sure he and his wife love you," Celia smiled.

Mandie suddenly jumped up. "Uncle Wirt," she said. "Would you please take me by Uncle Wirt's on the way back to Uncle Ned's?" she asked Riley. "He's the one who tried to keep this a secret from me. I want to talk to him now."

"All right, I'll take you by Uncle Wirt's, but let's don't go rushing off," Riley said. Looking at Joe and Celia, he added, "I think we should all sit down and have another cup of coffee, and I do believe I have some cookies left."

"Sounds good to me," Joe agreed.

"Yes," Celia added.

There was still enough coffee in the percolator for the three of them, and they sat at a small table in Riley's room and drank the coffee and finished the cookies. By then Mandie had calmed down.

"I believe I have a bag large enough to put that quilt in," Riley said, getting up to go look in a cabinet. He took a large feed bag from a shelf inside. "This ought to be large enough."

He carefully rolled up the quilt and stuffed it into the bag while the others watched.

"I'm ready," Mandie said, standing up.

"Mandie, I'm going to say something to you that Uncle Ned always says," Joe said as he followed her out of the schoolhouse. "Think before you act. Think how much all your Cherokee kin-people love you. That's why they didn't want you hurt by the message on the quilt. Think about that before you confront Uncle Wirt."

Mandie knew Joe was right, but she wouldn't admit it. "I'll see what he has to say," she said.

And she did wonder exactly what she would say to Uncle Wirt and what he would have to say to her. She knew he was known for his loud voice and his stubborn ways. But she wanted to know the whole story about her grandmother and was determined to get it.

Chapter 12 / Home at Last

As Riley drove them to Uncle Wirt's house, Mandie held on to Snowball and finally remembered the strange quilt in her valise in Sallie's room.

"I suppose Tsa'ni was the one who switched the quilts," Mandie said. Looking at Riley, she explained, "My valise with this quilt in it disappeared from Sallie's room when I first came, and then yesterday my valise was back but with a strange quilt in it. So that must be the quilt Aunt Saphronia gave Tsa'ni to give you. I don't know how Tsa'ni managed to take my valise with the quilt in it."

"A lot of things he does can't be explained," Riley said. "But if you will give me the other quilt when we get back to Uncle Ned's, I'll take it home with me."

When they got to Uncle Wirt's house, Aunt Saphronia told Mandie that Wirt was at Ned's house.

"I wanted to see him about something. We're going home tomorrow," Mandie told the woman as she stood by the cart talking. Celia held Snowball.

Aunt Saphronia reached to hug Mandie. Mandie

stiffened at first, also angry with Aunt Saphronia, but then she thought better of it and decided quickly that Wirt was the boss and Saphronia was not to blame. She hugged her back.

"Come back soon," the old woman told her. "Love."

"Love," Mandie replied as she got back in the cart and Riley drove on down the road.

When they arrived at Uncle Ned's house, Mandie walked ahead of the others as they went in the back door. She was carrying the Cherokee quilt. Celia held on to Snowball and finally put him down. He ran to the woodbox. Sallie was studying the books at one end of the long table. Uncle Ned and Uncle Wirt were drinking coffee at the other end. Morning Star was stirring pots on the cookstove.

"I am glad to see you back," Sallie greeted them as she closed her books.

No one spoke. Mandie walked directly to Uncle Wirt, pulled the quilt out of the feed bag and shook it out. "This says that the woman who married my grandfather hated white people and that they should all be killed," she yelled at the old man.

Wirt and Ned both jumped to their feet. Mandie's friends stayed by the doorway. Sallie and Morning Star said something hurriedly in Cherokee as they backed away from Mandie.

"Yes, that what say!" Uncle Wirt yelled back at Mandie.

"Where you get quilt?" Uncle Ned demanded in a loud voice, something unusual for him.

"Why did y'all keep this a secret from me? This woman married my grandfather, and I have a right to know what she was like," Mandie screamed back.

Joe crept through the crowd and came to

Mandie's side. He grasped her hand and yanked as he whispered, "Think before acting."

Mandie took a deep breath and said in a calmer voice, "I want to know why y'all have been keeping secrets from me. Tell me. Now." She looked from Uncle Ned to Uncle Wirt and watched them closely as they glanced at each other.

"Not want to hurt," Uncle Ned finally spoke.

"Message not truth. Message a lie," Uncle Wirt told her.

"What do you mean, the message is a lie?" Mandie demanded. Joe still held one of her hands.

"Talitha love your grandfather, and he white man," Uncle Wirt said sadly.

"Then why did she put a message on here that all white people in Cherokee country should be killed?" Mandie asked, shaking the quilt at him.

"Quilt made before Talitha meet your grandfather," Uncle Ned tried to explain. "Your grandfather make secret tunnel to save his Cherokee friends. Talitha stayed in tunnel to be safe. Where you get quilt?"

"Tsa'ni gave this quilt to Riley O'Neal and said Aunt Saphronia sent it," Mandie explained. "And where did Tsa'ni get the quilt? I brought it with me when I came here. It was in a valise in Sallie's room, and it disappeared, valise and all. Then the valise came back with another quilt in it. I want to know what's going on."

"I tell you truth, Papoose," Uncle Ned said. "How this happen. I took quilt in your valise because I take quilt back to John Shaw's house and tell you to put away and you do not. I put in my room and it go away. Now I see Tsa'ni must find it and take it."

"Uncle Ned! You took the quilt?" Mandie was

crying by this time. "How could you do that?"

Joe moved closer and put an arm around Mandie. He whispered to Celia by her side, "Please go upstairs and get the other quilt."

"All right," Celia replied and hurried from the room.

"Yes, I take quilt," Uncle Ned said firmly. "Quilt not belong to Papoose. Quilt belong to John Shaw. I will take to John Shaw, was his mother's."

Mandie was shocked with the remark, that she did not own the quilt, that it was her uncle's property. "But I found the quilt in the attic," Mandie argued.

"John Shaw know quilt in attic. He know message on quilt," Uncle Ned replied. "He know his mother made another quilt when she met his father, and it has love sewn into it."

"Uncle John knew about this quilt? And he has another one his mother made? He never told me," Mandie argued.

Uncle Ned stepped forward and reached out to take the quilt. Mandie jumped away from him and squeezed the quilt in her arms.

"No, no, it's mine!" she declared.

Uncle Ned was shocked with her behavior. He said, "I promise Jim Shaw I watch over Papoose, but Papoose not want me." He sat down at the table and bowed his head.

Mandie felt her blue eyes flood with tears, and she started to reach out to the old man. But then she quickly changed her mind. He was in the plan to keep her from knowing anything about the quilt. Breaking loose from Joe's grasp on her arm, Mandie rushed out the back door and ran into the yard to a fallen log, where she sat down and collapsed.

"Mandie," Joe said, catching up with her and

sitting on the log. "Come on. Let's go for a walk so we can talk." He reached for her hand, and she didn't pull away. Instead she clutched the quilt with the other hand as she got to her feet.

Joe, holding tightly to her hand, led the way slowly down to the road. They walked and walked, silently, for a long time.

All the time, Mandie was trying to sort things out in her head. She knew she had hurt Uncle Ned, and she knew she had done a great wrong. But how was she ever going to straighten things out? Would he ever forgive her?

Finally Joe spoke. "Here comes Dimar," he said, motioning toward the approaching cart.

"Dimar," Mandie repeated as the cart met them and stopped in the road.

"Where are you going?" Dimar asked, jumping down from the cart.

"No place really, just walking," Joe replied, glancing at Mandie.

"I was coming to Uncle Ned's house to ask if you would like to go hunting tomorrow," Dimar said.

"Thank you, Dimar, but we are leaving early tomorrow morning," Joe told him.

"I am sorry to see you go," Dimar answered. "Will you come back again this summer?"

"I don't know," Joe said, glancing at Mandie.

"We are going to New York when we get back to my house, but I don't know what we will do the rest of our vacation," Mandie told him. The quilt was heavy in her arms as she tried to roll it up.

"If you are ready to go back, I would be glad for you to ride in my cart with that quilt," Dimar offered.

Mandie quickly made a decision. She couldn't

run away forever. "Yes, Dimar, thank you, we will go back," Mandie replied.

Joe looked at her but didn't say anything as he helped her into Dimar's cart.

As they rode back to Uncle Ned's house, Mandie did a lot of thinking while Joe and Dimar discussed hunting. She silently asked God to forgive her and to show her the way to straighten matters out. But when Dimar turned the cart into Uncle Ned's yard, Mandie still didn't know what to do.

"Come on, let's go inside," Joe said, helping Mandie out of the cart with the quilt. "Dimar, you are coming in, too, aren't you?"

"Yes, for a few minutes," Dimar agreed.

The three walked through the back door. Mandie saw that everyone was still there but no one seemed to be talking. She hesitated for a moment and then ran to the huge open fireplace. She took a deep breath and tossed the quilt into the flames. There was a loud explosion as it caught fire.

Mandie turned to go to Uncle Ned, but he had come to her. The old man held her tightly and smoothed her hair while she cried.

"I'm sorry, Uncle Ned, please forgive me," she begged.

"Problem gone, up in fire," the old man said. "Love, Papoose."

"I love you so much, Uncle Ned," Mandie whispered to him. She turned to look at the fire. The quilt was burning rapidly, burning away all the hard feelings associated with it.

"Sit. Coffee," Morning Star called from across the room.

Mandie laughed and said, "Morning Star thinks coffee is a cure for everything." She wiped her eyes with the back of her hand and turned to face her friends. At that moment everyone clapped.

"Mystery solved," Joe said.

"Problems solved," Celia added.

As Mandie walked over to the table, she realized Aunt Saphronia was sitting by Uncle Wirt. The old woman had not been there when she ran out of the house.

"I bring love," Aunt Saphronia told her as she rose from the table and held up a brightly colored quilt.

"Oh, what a beautiful quilt," Mandie said, going to look at it.

"This message of love," Aunt Saphronia explained, pointing to the birds and flowers on the quilt. "Talitha make this for her white husband. It says love." She held the quilt out for Mandie to take.

Mandie hesitated for a moment. "But that is not mine," she said.

"Mine. I give you," Aunt Saphronia tried to explain.

"Yours? But I don't understand," Mandie said, still not touching the quilt.

"I help Talitha make when marry. When Talitha go to other world, John Shaw give me," the old woman said. "Please take."

"Uncle John gave you this quilt?" Mandie repeated.

"Because I help make," Aunt Saphronia replied. "Now I give you."

"Oh, Aunt Saphronia, I love you," Mandie exclaimed as she hugged the little old lady, quilt and all. Then straightening up, she accepted the quilt.

"Sit. Coffee," Morning Star kept insisting.

When everyone sat down at the long table,

Riley was across from Mandie. "Celia gave me the quilt you had in your valise, and Uncle Wirt went to get Aunt Saphronia to be sure it was the quilt she had given Tsa'ni for me. And guess what? It was."

"I'm glad you've finally got yourself a new quilt," Mandie said, smiling across the table.

"And I'm glad you got yourself a new quilt with a beautiful message," Riley replied.

Mandie looked at the quilt she had draped across the back of her chair. She thought it was the most beautiful quilt she had ever seen.

―――――――

That night Mandie slept soundly and didn't even dream.

The next morning she was up before daylight. She was anxious to get home now that the quilt mystery had been solved. She could hardly wait to go on to New York from there and tell Uncle John Shaw what had happened.

Uncle Ned drove the wagon faster than usual, and they didn't take time for any rest stops.

"We hurry," Uncle Ned explained as they went over the mountain. "I go back home today, not spend night."

Mandie, holding Snowball, said, "We're in a hurry anyhow. We'd like to go on to New York tomorrow if Grandmother is agreeable."

"I don't believe she is in any hurry to go to New York, or I should say, to Lindall Guyer's house in New York," Joe said.

"There is something rather unusual about that, isn't there?" Celia said.

"I don't understand why she is going to the man's house if she doesn't really like him," Mandie pondered.

"Miz Taft know Mr. Guyer long time ago," Uncle Ned told them.

"A long time ago? How long ago, Uncle Ned?" Mandie asked.

"Many years ago when Mr. Taft living, Mr. Guyer come visit their house," Uncle Ned explained.

"In other words, Mr. Guyer knew Grandfather Taft, too," Mandie said. "That is very interesting."

"Mandie, I can see you are getting involved in another mystery," Joe said with a big grin.

"Someday I'll figure all this out," Mandie said, sighing.

When Uncle Ned pulled his wagon up in the Shaws' driveway a while later, Mandie was surprised to see Dr. Woodard's buggy there.

"Joe, I wonder if your mother and father have come to go with us to visit my Cherokee kinpeople, not knowing we've already been there," Mandie said as everyone stepped down from the wagon.

Mandie held on to her white cat, and Celia carried the quilt for her. Uncle Ned and Joe carried their bags.

They met up with Dr. Woodard in the front hallway.

"We figured y'all would return today," Dr. Woodard told them.

"Are you going to New York with us?" Mandie asked, setting Snowball down.

"Yes, we thought we'd go up for a few days," Dr. Woodard replied. "I'd like to talk to Dr. Plumbley and see what's new in the medical field."

"I'm glad," Joe said with a smile for his father.

As Mandie took the quilt from Celia, Dr. Woodard stepped over to look at it. "That's a beautiful quilt you've got there. Any chance it might be for sale?" he asked Mandie.

"No, sir, all the gold in the world couldn't buy this quilt," Mandie replied with a big grin. "You see, my Grandmother Shaw made it." Then, turning to Celia, she winked at her friend and added, "Now, Dr. Woodard, Celia and I are learning to make something called the Album Block. We'd be glad to make one for you."

Dr. Woodard smiled back and said, "If you ever get it down, let me take a look at it."

Mrs. Taft came into the hallway at that moment. She came to embrace Mandie. "I'm so glad you came home today. We can go on to New York tomorrow."

"You sound like you're in a hurry to go," Mandie said with a big grin.

Mrs. Taft frowned and said, "Might as well go on and get it over with so we can do other things."

"Other things?" Mandie questioned.

"Perhaps we will visit the Pattons in Charleston," Mrs. Taft replied. "And Senator Morton is coming through here after we return from New York." She walked on down the hallway and went into the back parlor.

Mandie and Celia looked at each other and burst out laughing.

"I knew Grandmother was going to have some plans of her own," Mandie said with a laugh. "This may be a very interesting summer."

COMING NEXT!
MANDIE AND THE NEW YORK SECRET
(MANDIE BOOK/36)

A secret from the past is solved.

Win an Autographed MANDIE BOOK

The first one hundred readers who fill out and send in the following will receive a free autographed copy of MANDIE BOOK #36, *Mandie and the New York Secret*, to be published in early 2003. If you need more space, add an extra sheet of paper.

This is the thirty-fifth MANDIE BOOK, and Mandie has aged only four years since book #1. What should happen to Mandie next?

Would you like for Mandie to grow up?

What kind of work should she do?

Should she marry?

What place should she visit next?

Where should she go to college?

What do you like about Mandie?

Who is your favorite character other than Mandie?

Which is your favorite MANDIE BOOK? Why?

Have you learned any lessons from Mandie?

Are you a member of the Mandie Fan Club?

When we receive the first one hundred replies to this questionnaire, we will let you know at *www.Mandie.com* and will mail book #36 to the winners.

Mail this questionnaire to:
    Lois Gladys Leppard
    % Bethany House Publishers
    11400 Hampshire Avenue South
    Bloomington, Minnesota 55438

Mandie's Album Block
Instructions by Stephanie Whitson

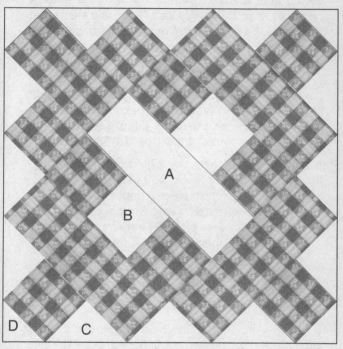

Diagram not drawn to scale.

Note: This pattern assumes you will be sewing "Mandie's way"—by hand.

Step 1: Gather supplies:

fabric scissors

sharpened lead pencil

card stock for pattern pieces

scraps of a 100% cotton print fabric

scraps of muslin (off-white)

needle appropriate for hand sewing

thimble (optional)

cotton thread—ivory

Step 2: Make the pattern:

The pattern pieces on pages 157 and 159 are printed *exactly* the right size, *including* seam allowance. You will *cut* on the solid line and *sew* on the dotted line. It is very important that your pattern pieces be *exactly* the right size. When you are tracing the pieces, be very careful not to make them bigger or smaller. Even a small error in this step will cause problems later.

Carefully cut out the pattern pieces printed on pages 157 and 159. Cut along the *inside* of the dark line. Using a sharp pencil, trace around these pieces onto card stock, and then cut the pieces out. These are the pattern pieces you will use for Step 3.

Step 3: Trace around the pieces you made in Step 2 onto the right side of your fabric. You will need

    1 rectangle (pattern piece A) from muslin
    4 rectangles (pattern piece A) from print fabric
    2 squares (pattern piece B) from muslin
    14 squares (pattern piece B) from print fabric
    12 large triangles (pattern piece C) from muslin
    4 small triangles (pattern piece D) from muslin

When you have the pieces traced onto the fabric, carefully cut them out.

Step 4: Draw the sewing line ¼ inch from the edge of each piece of fabric you cut in Step 3. Draw this line on the *wrong* side of the fabric.

Step 5: Assemble each section of the album block.

Take one print square B and one muslin square B. With *right* sides of the fabric facing each other, pin the two squares together so that the dotted lines match exactly. Stitch along the dotted line using a small running stitch (just in-and-out, in-and-out along the dotted line). Every few stitches take a back stitch to make the seam stronger. Take another print square B and pin and stitch it to the other side of the muslin square just as you did with the first. Press the seams toward the *printed* fabric. Don't skip pressing; it's important. NOTE: Quilters do *not* press seams open.

You have now made the shaded section of the block:

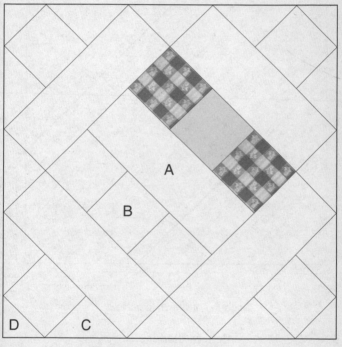

Diagram not drawn to scale.

Study the above diagram and make the rest of the sections. Always try to press seams toward the print fabric.

Step 6: Join units 1, 2, and 3 (see diagram below). Press your finished quilt block.

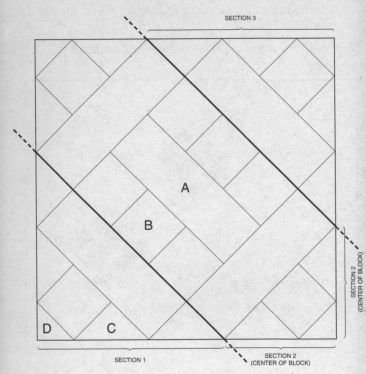

Diagram not drawn to scale.

Congratulations!

You've just made Mandie's Album Block! Girls who made Album quilts long ago often had their friends sign the rectangle in the center. If you want to sign your block, use a permanent ink pen designed especially for fabric.

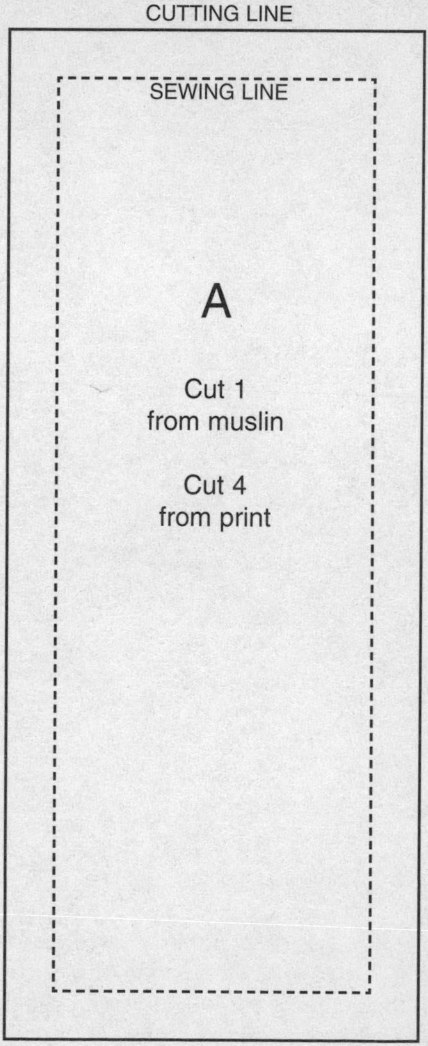

CUTTING LINE

SEWING LINE

A

Cut 1
from muslin

Cut 4
from print

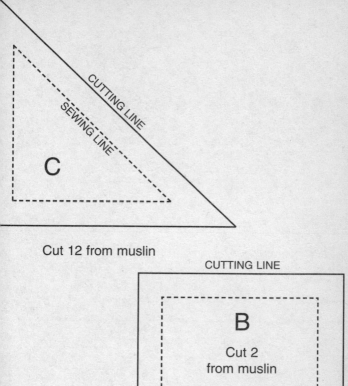

CUTTING LINE

SEWING LINE

C

Cut 12 from muslin

CUTTING LINE

B

Cut 2
from muslin

Cut 14
from print

SEWING LINE

CUTTING LINE

SEWING LINE

D

Cut 4 from muslin